MRS. JEFFRIES
WEEDS THE PLOT

MRS. JEFFRIES
WEEDS THE PLOT

Emily Brightwell

Thorndike Press • **Chivers Press**
Waterville, Maine USA Bath, England

This Large Print edition is published by Thorndike Press, USA and by Chivers Press, England.

Published in 2002 in the U.S. by The Berkley Publishing Group, a member of Penguin Putnam Inc.

Published in 2002 in the U.K. by arrangement with The Berkley Publishing Group, a member of Penguin Putnam Inc.

U.S. Softcover 0-7862-4464-X (Paperback Series)
U.K. Hardcover 0-7540-7493-5 (Chivers Large Print)
U.K. Softcover 0-7540-7494-3 (Camden Large Print)

The text of this Large Print edition is unabridged.
Other aspects of the book may vary from the original edition.

Set in 16 pt. Plantin by Minnie B. Raven.

Printed in the United States on permanent paper.

British Library Cataloguing-in-Publication Data available

Library of Congress Cataloging-in-Publication Data

Brightwell, Emily.
    Mrs. Jeffries weeds the plot / Emily Brightwell.
       p. cm.
    ISBN 0-7862-4464-X (lg. print : sc : alk. paper)
    1. Jeffries, Mrs. (Fictitious character) — Fiction.
    2. Witherspoon, Gerald (Fictitious character) — Fiction.
    3. Police — England — Fiction. 4. Women domestics —
Fiction. 5. Large type books. I. Title.
PS3552.R46443 M77 2002
    823′.914—dc21
                                        2002028425

To Ann Ruggles,
with my heartfelt thanks and gratitude for
answering all my questions about dogs.

And to Oreo, Abby, and Clancy,
with thanks for the great stories
and the good laughs.

Chapter 1

"Really, I honestly don't know why Louisa won't believe me. I'm not making it up," Annabeth Gentry said to her maid. She was an attractive, blond woman in her late thirties. Her eyes were bright blue and she possessed a cheerful disposition and, usually, a ready smile. She wasn't smiling now.

"Of course you're not making it up, ma'am," her maid, Martha Dowling, replied. She put the tray she'd been carrying down on a table by the window and poured her mistress a cup of tea.

"I'm not usually in the habit of telling tales, am I?" Annabeth got up and began to pace the small sitting room.

"No, ma'am. Did Mrs. Cooksey actually say she thought you was lyin'?" Martha asked.

Annabeth stopped in front of the fireplace. "She didn't come right out and accuse me of making it up, but I could tell by the expression on her face that she didn't take my concerns seriously." Her shoulders slumped. "She thinks I'm getting fanciful.

She said that unmarried women get funny ideas in their heads when they get to be my age."

"That's the silliest bit of nonsense I've ever heard," Martha snorted, handing the tea to her mistress. "You're one of the most sensible people I've ever met." She wasn't at all afraid of being reprimanded for her bluntness. Unlike most women of her class, Miss Gentry wasn't one to get annoyed over an honest answer.

"But it wasn't just Louisa," Annabeth wailed. She put the tea down on the mantel and began pacing again. "It was Reverend Cooksey, too. Now that the fuss about Miranda finding that body has died down, he thinks I miss being the center of attention."

"That's even sillier than Mrs. Cooksey's notion that you're getting strange fancies. It weren't your fault Miranda dug up that corpse. You didn't ask all them newspapers to interview you and put your name in the papers." Martha shook her head in disgust. She thought both the Cookseys fools. "I don't mean to be steppin' out of my place, ma'am, but you need help. You've almost been run down by a carriage, clouted on the head with a load of flyin' bricks, and someone's even tried to poison you. And that's just been in the last two weeks. You can't go on like this, ma'am. Whoever's doin' all this is goin' to get lucky soon and you're goin' to end up pushing up daisies."

"You believe me, then?" Annabeth asked quietly. "You don't think I'm making things up to get attention or that it's all my imagination?"

"Of course I believe you, ma'am," Martha replied. "I was there when them bricks come topplin' off the top of the garden wall and I was there when poor Miranda keeled over after she ate part of your scone. Good thing she didn't take more than a bite or she'd be a goner."

Annabeth shuddered. "That was a dreadful day." She glanced at the bloodhound. Miranda was lying in a shaft of sunlight streaming in through the lace curtains, enjoying the warm September sunshine.

"You'll not get any argument from me, ma'am. Pardon the expression, but poor Miranda was as sick as a dog. Of course, she *is* a dog, but she did look pitiful."

Hearing her name bandied about, Miranda raised her head and looked at the two women.

"We've got to do something, ma'am," Martha continued earnestly, "and we must do it quickly."

"You think I ought to go to the police?" Annabeth picked up her teacup and took a quick sip.

"That'll not do any good without proof, ma'am. If your own family won't believe you, you don't have much chance of convincin' the coppers."

"Then I don't see what I can do." Annabeth sighed heavily. "It's hopeless. I was so looking forward to moving into my new home, too. Now it appears as if I ought to move away, far away. Then maybe whoever is trying to kill me will give up."

Martha, being from a far less protected class than Miss Gentry, knew better than that. " 'Course they won't, they'll just follow you. Mark my words, ma'am, if someone's wantin' to do you in, they'll only stop if you're six feet under or if you catch 'em first."

Annabeth's eyes widened. "Oh dear, I don't want to die. There are so many places I want to go. I've always wanted to travel, you know —"

"You're not goin' to die," Martha interrupted. When she was excited, her accent tended to revert to the one she'd been born to, not the one she'd acquired working as a ladies' maid. "We're goin' to catch the villain, that's what we're goin' to do. I

10

think I know someone who could help."

"Help how?"

"Help by finding out who's trying to do you in, ma'am." Martha grinned. "Her name is Betsy. She's very good at detecting stuff, and even better, she works for Inspector Gerald Witherspoon of Scotland Yard. I know Betsy'll believe us, and what's more, she'll be able to do something about it."

Annabeth frowned in confusion. "She works for a police inspector?"

"She's his maid, ma'am, but don't let that fool you. She's also a right good snoop. Now, you just leave everything to me. We'll have you safe and sound in no time."

Mrs. Goodge, the cook, put the big brown teapot on the table next to a plate of buttered bread. She was a portly, gray-haired woman who'd cooked for some of the finest families in all of England. She now cooked for Inspector Gerald Witherspoon of Scotland Yard and she wouldn't have given up working for him to be the head cook at Buckingham Palace. Indeed she wouldn't.

"Are the others coming?" Betsy, the blond-haired maid, asked as she stepped into the kitchen. She smiled at the housekeeper and the cook.

Mrs. Jeffries, the housekeeper, smiled back. "Wiggins went to wash his hands. I haven't seen Smythe since breakfast, but I'm assuming he'll be here at the usual time. Do you have any idea where he's got to this morning?"

Betsy knew good and well where Smythe had gone, but she didn't really want to mention it to the others. Drat, this was awkward. The cook and the housekeeper were watching her inquiringly. "I think he went to the stables," she mumbled as she sat down. She hated telling lies. But she could hardly admit that her fiancé had gone to see his banker to check about his investments. Not when the rest of the household thought he was just a simple coachman. Drat, Smythe *was* a coachman, of course. He just happened to be a very rich one.

"I expect he'll be back shortly," Mrs. Jeffries said briskly. She was a motherly, plump woman dressed in a brown bombazine dress. She had dark brown eyes and auburn hair lightly streaked with gray. She smiled easily and often.

"Cor blimey, I'm starvin'." Wiggins, the apple-cheeked footman, rushed into the room and plopped down next to the cook. "Do we have to wait for Smythe? I've got

12

ever so much to do this mornin'. I know it's warm outside, but it's already September and I want to get another coat of paint on the back windowsills before the cold sets in."

"Help yourself to something to eat," the housekeeper said as she began pouring the tea. "I'm sure Smythe won't mind if we start without him."

"What else do you have to do today?" the cook asked the footman. She eyed him suspiciously. She had a few chores in mind for the lad. The wet larder could use a good scrubbing, for example.

"After I finish the paintin' " — Wiggins stuffed a bite of bread into his mouth — "I was goin' to pop 'round and show Horace, Lady Cannonberry's footman, how to mix that new polish for the door brasses."

"That sounds like a very good idea," Mrs. Jeffries said. "Is Lady Cannonberry still gone?" Their neighbor, Ruth Cannonberry, was a good friend and she was also very special to Inspector Witherspoon.

"She's coming back on the fifteenth," Wiggins replied. He turned his head and glanced toward the hall as the back door opened. The soft murmur of voices and the sound of footsteps echoed clearly in the quiet kitchen.

"That's Smythe," Betsy said. She easily recognized his voice.

"He's got someone with him," Mrs. Goodge added.

"It's a woman," Betsy mumbled.

A moment later, the coachman, accompanied by a stranger, stepped into the kitchen. Smythe was a tall, muscular fellow with dark brown hair and heavy, rather brutal features. He smiled broadly as he spotted Betsy sitting at the kitchen table. "This young lady wants to 'ave a word with you," he said to her.

Betsy studied his companion. She was a tall, big-boned woman in her early twenties with dark hair and hazel eyes. She wore a pale lavender broadcloth dress and a short, thin brown jacket. The slender face under the serviceable broad-brimmed hat seemed vaguely familiar. Betsy didn't know who she was, yet the girl was smiling at her like they were old friends. "I'm sorry," Betsy said, "have we met before?"

"It's been a few years," the girl replied, "and I've filled out a bit. My name is Martha Dowling and we met when you come around to Mayfair when I worked for Mr. Vincent. Remember, you pretended to run into me accidentally like so you could ask me all them questions."

"Oh yes." Betsy grinned as she remembered. "Of course. You worked for Justin Vincent. Sad how that turned out."

Martha shrugged philosophically. "It couldn't be helped."

"How nice to see you again," Betsy said quickly. "Won't you sit down?" She gestured toward an empty chair.

"Thanks all the same," Martha replied. "But if it's all right with your housekeeper" — she nodded respectfully at Mrs. Jeffries — "I'd like to have word with you in private. It's a rather delicate matter, you see." She smiled nervously.

Betsy had an idea of why the woman had come. Apparently, she hadn't been as discreet with her investigating back in those days as she'd hoped. "A delicate matter? Does that mean you need my help?" she asked bluntly. "The kind of help you're not wanting to go to the police about, I suppose." She was relieved to think that was the reason Smythe had brought the woman inside. She trusted him, of course. But she was glad to know that Martha had come here to see her and wasn't someone from her fiancé's past.

The girl cast a quick, wary look at the others sitting around the table. "Uh . . . well . . ."

"Don't worry. You can speak in front of them." Betsy gestured at the others. "They know all about the circumstances of our last meeting. We have no secrets here." Except about money, she thought, glancing at Smythe, who looked away.

"It's all right, my dear," Mrs. Jeffries said kindly. She deliberately kept her tone informal. "If you're in some sort of trouble —"

"It's not me," Martha exclaimed quickly. "It's me mistress."

Mrs. Jeffries knew the others sensed an adventure in the making. Mrs. Goodge leaned forward with her head slightly cocked to the left so she could hear every word (Mrs. Jeffries suspected she'd gone a tad deaf in her right ear). Smythe, who'd been in the midst of taking his seat, went stock-still, and Wiggins had actually pulled his hand back from reaching for a slice of bread. Oh yes, Mrs. Jeffries thought, they'd caught the scent all right.

"What's wrong with yer mistress?" Wiggins asked. " 'As she gone missin' or is someone tryin' to 'urt 'er?"

Martha gasped. "How'd you know?"

"We knows lots of things," Wiggins told her confidently. He patted the empty chair on his other side. "You come and 'ave a

16

sit-down next to me. We'll get everything sorted out as right as rain."

Martha smiled in relief and sat down next to the lad.

Mrs. Jeffries quickly poured the girl a cup of tea. "Here, my dear. Have some refreshment. Then tell us what this is all about. Take your time."

"Ta." Martha's gaze darted quickly around the table over the top of the cup as she took a sip. "I'm not sure where to begin."

"Why don't you begin at the beginning?" Mrs. Goodge suggested. "That's always best."

"That's right," Wiggins added. "That's where I always like to start." He was eager to know everything about Martha. She was a bit taller than he and a bit older, but she was pretty.

"Right, then." Martha took a long, deep breath and sat her cup down. "I work for a lady named Annabeth Gentry. We live at number seventeen Orley Road in Hammersmith. It's a quiet life — well, usually it's quiet. Mind you, people did make a bit of fuss when Miranda and Miss Gentry got in the newspapers for finding that body. But that's passed and we're back to doin' what we always did. At least we were until bricks come flyin' off the wall and poison ended up in the scones —"

"Body?" Wiggins interrupted. "What body? And who's Miranda?"

The others were all staring intently at the girl.

"Oh, Miranda is Miss Gentry's dog," Martha said proudly. "She's a bloodhound. She's got the best nose in all of England. Miss Gentry has taught her to do all kinds of interestin' things. I don't think she quite had diggin' up dead bodies in mind when she was teachin' the pup all those tricks, but there you have it. Life's like that, innit? You never know what's going to happen. Here she and Miranda was just out doin' a bit of trainin' and all of a sudden the pup starts diggin' like a mad thing, and before you know it, Miranda had dug up that corpse."

"Miss Dowling, I'm sorry, please slow down. I'm afraid I'm getting confused," Mrs. Jeffries said softly. "You're going too quickly for me to take this all in. Are you saying someone is trying to kill Miss Gentry because her dog dug up a body?"

"Oh, no." Martha waved her hand in dismissal. "I'm sorry, I didn't mean to ramble on and on. I tend to do that when I'm nervous." She paused and took a deep breath. "Let me start again. Someone's trying to kill my mistress, but I don't think it has anything to do with Miranda finding that poor man's body. The police think whoever killed him and planted him on the side of the path is long gone."

"Do they know who he was?" Smythe asked.

Martha nodded. "Feller named Tim Porter. He were well known to the police. Been in and out of knick all the time for pickin' pockets and petty stuff like that."

The coachman made a mental note to have a good look into the circumstances of Porter's death. Despite what the girl said, he thought the attempts on this Miss Gentry's life might have a lot to do with finding a body.

"How was the man killed?" Mrs. Goodge pushed the plate of bread and butter toward the girl. "Help yourself."

"Ta," Martha said as she grabbed a slice. "The police said his throat had been slit." She took a bite of the bread. "But like I said, I don't think that could have anything to do with Miss Gentry's troubles. It weren't like Miranda was sniffin' about for the one that did the killin'. She just found the corpse."

"How long after discovering the body did the attempts on Miss Gentry's life begin?" Mrs. Jeffries asked.

Martha thought for a moment. "Let me see now. It would have been a week or so later. Yes, yes." She nodded eagerly, "That's right. Miranda found the body on August tenth and the attempts started about the seventeenth. I remember because the first one was the same day that Miss Gentry went to afternoon tea at her sister's house in Kensington. When she was on her way home, someone tried to run her down in a carriage. Right on the corner of the Brompton Road it was, and no one saw a bloomin' thing neither. Everyone said it happened too fast."

Wiggins's eyes were big as saucers. "What saved her?"

"She's a strong woman, is Miss Gentry. When she saw that coach-and-four bearin' down on her, she gave one almightly leap onto the pavement. Landed on her knees and scraped 'em real bad she did, but she was safe. The carriage kept on goin' down the Brompton Road."

"Could it have been an accident?" Mrs. Jeffries inquired. Before they got their hopes up, she wanted to be absolutely sure there really was something to investigate.

"At first we thought that's exactly what it was," Martha said earnestly. "You don't expect to get knocked about when you're walkin' in Kensington in broad daylight, do you? But when the other things started happening, that's when Miss Gentry got to thinking that the coach accident was no accident, if you get my meaning."

"Tell us about the other things." Betsy picked up her own cup and took a quick sip.

"A day or so after she was almost run down, a bunch of bricks come tumbling off the top of the garden wall right onto the spot where Miss Gentry was sittin'. Her head would've been crushed exceptin' for the fact that not two seconds before it happened, she dropped her spoon under the table and bent down to pick it up. It was the table that kept her from bein' coshed. As it was, she got her arm bruised pretty badly."

"Did anyone see who did it?" Smythe asked.

"No, more's the pity," Martha said. "It's a ten-foot wall, and by the time we'd rounded up the lad from next door to skivvy over and see what was what, there was no one there. But there was a ladder lying on the ground close by."

"That's a rather peculiar way to try and kill someone," Mrs. Jeffries mused. "How could the assailant know that Miss Gentry would be sitting in the, well . . . right spot?"

"It's where she always sat for tea," Martha exclaimed. "If the sun was shinin', she had tea there every day. Besides, it weren't one brick that come tumbling down, it were a whole lot of 'em. That's how come Miss Gentry got her arm bruised. When she realized what was happening she squeezed under the table, but she weren't quick enough to get her whole body under it."

"Maybe the mortar just come loose," Wiggins suggested.

"Them bricks had been pried loose," Martha insisted. "We went 'round to the school and had a look ourselves later that day."

"So it's a school yard on the other side," the cook said brightly. "That explains it, then; it was probably some silly schoolboy prank that went wrong."

"The school closed down right after Easter. There was no one there but the caretaker and he'd been taking a nap. Looked like someone had spent the better part of that Sunday afternoon chiseling the mortar out of them bricks and then waitin' till Miss Gentry was sittin' down in her spot before they pushed 'em over. You can take a look, the tea table is right beside that wall. If Miss Gentry hadn't reached for that spoon, she'd have been a goner."

Mrs. Jeffries leaned forward. "I'm sure you're right, my dear. Now, what about the scones being poisoned?"

"Not the scones, the cream." Martha sighed. "Mind you, Miranda'd be dead, too, if that fat old cat from down the street hadn't come into the garden and caught her attention before she ate the rest of Miss Gentry's scone."

"So it was the cream that was poisoned?" Mrs. Jeffries clarified. This was a most bizarre tale, but she'd learned in her life that merely because circumstances sounded odd didn't make them any less true.

"Right. There were just a thin layer spread on Miss Gentry's scone, she's not all that fond of it. But we'd run out of butter, so she used the cream . . . we were havin' guests that day and it were a good thing Miranda snatched that bite first and got sick, otherwise we'd have had a houseful of dead guests . . ." Her voice trailed off as she took in their expressions. Everyone looked thoroughly confused. "Look, I'm not explainin' things very well . . ."

"That's not true," Wiggins protested. "You're doin' a right good job if you ask me."

She flashed the footman a grateful smile. "That's kind of you to say, but the truth is, Miss Gentry could tell it all much better than me. I was wonderin' if I could bring her 'round this afternoon."

"I think that's a splendid idea," Mrs. Jeffries said quickly. She darted a fast look around the table; the others were nodding their agreement and she suspected they were thinking the same thing she was. By the time Martha and her mistress came back today, they could verify a number of things. "We'd be pleased to meet Miss Gentry and hear her story."

Martha smiled gratefully. "That's ever so wonderful. This is such a load off of my mind, it is."

"Why didn't you go to the police after the dog was poisoned?" Mrs. Goodge asked curiously.

"The mistress and I thought about it," Martha answered. "But we had no proof."

"You had the poisoned cream," Smythe pointed out softly.

"No, we didn't," Martha said. "When Miss Gentry and I went back out to the terrace after taking care of Miranda and

24

getting rid of everyone, the cream pot was gone. That's how we knew it was poison! As I've said, my mistress can explain everything much better than I can."

"Actually," Mrs. Jeffries said quickly, "I do believe it would be best if one of us came to see you. Would Miss Gentry be available tomorrow morning?"

Martha's brow furrowed in confusion. Then she shrugged. "To get some help, she'll be available anytime you want. Tomorrow will be fine. What time?"

"Ten o'clock."

Martha stood up. She still looked a bit puzzled by the sudden change of plans, but apparently had decided to leave well enough alone.

"Before you go," Mrs. Jeffries said, "there's just one or two more questions we'd like to ask. It'll only take a moment."

"All right." Martha sat down and the housekeeper finished her questions. A few minutes later, Betsy escorted the girl to the back door.

As soon as the two women were out of sight, Smythe was on his feet and looking inquiringly at the housekeeper. She nodded and he disappeared in the opposite direction, up the stairs leading to the front door.

"You havin' Smythe follow her?" Wiggins asked in a loud whisper. He looked very disappointed. He'd have liked that job himself.

"I think that's best, don't you?" the housekeeper said quietly. "It'll give him the opportunity to see the layout of Miss Gentry's home firsthand."

"Why didn't he just offer to take her back himself?" Wiggins asked curiously. He wasn't quite as cynical as the others; he actually believed what people told him.

"Because we want to see for ourselves what's what," the cook said impatiently. "Following her will give Smythe a good chance to take the lay of the land, have a nice look around, and see just how far that wall actually is from the tea table."

"And sendin' her off like that'll give us a chance to find out if that dog really did find a dead body," Wiggins finished. He leapt to his feet, scooting the chair back loudly against the floor as he did so. "I can nip down to the station and have a word with Constable Griffiths. He'll know if some dog dug up a body."

"Mind how you talk to him," Betsy warned as she came back to the kitchen. Constable Griffiths had worked on a number of the inspector's cases. This

26

wouldn't be the first time they'd used him for information. "He's no fool."

"Should we send someone to fetch Luty and Hatchet?" Mrs. Goodge asked.

Mrs. Jeffries considered the question. Luty Belle Crookshank and her butler, Hatchet, would be very annoyed to be kept out of an investigation. They were good friends of the household of Upper Edmonton Gardens and always helped with the inspector's cases. "I'm not sure we ought to involve them until we know for certain we've got something to investigate."

"Are you sure, Mrs. Jeffries?" Betsy pressed. "They'll both get their noses out of joint if they find out we've started snooping without them."

Mrs. Jeffries considered the maid's warning. "You're right, of course." She sighed. "They will be annoyed. But what if this is only a tempest in a teapot? What if this Miss Gentry is one of those very unfortunate and rather pathetic people who make up stories to get a little attention?"

"If that were true, would her maid have come all this way to ask for our help?" Betsy asked. "She seems to like her mistress, but I don't think she'd go to all this trouble unless she was certain Miss Gentry was really in danger."

"Don't be too sure of that," Mrs. Goodge put in. "I've known some really silly women who had equally silly maids."

Betsy shook her head. "Martha figured out what I was up to when she worked for Vincent, so she can't be too silly." The moment the words were out, she clamped her lips shut, wishing she'd kept her comment to herself or just agreed with the cook. She didn't like reminding the others that she was the one who'd questioned Martha on that case. She was the one who'd been a lot less clever than she'd thought. They weren't supposed to let anyone know they helped Inspector Witherspoon. No one. But this girl had sussed it out and it had been all Betsy's fault.

"Don't worry about it, Betsy," Mrs. Jeffries said softly. "Sometimes it's impossible to get information out of people without giving the game away, so to speak."

Betsy's shoulders sagged in relief. "You're not annoyed about it?"

"Don't be daft, girl," the cook interjected. "Of course we're not. We've all had to tell more than we wanted every once in a while."

"Martha Dowling isn't the first person

to catch us out." Mrs. Jeffries smiled kindly. "And I doubt she'll be the last. Now stop fretting and let's have a good think about whether or not there's something else we can do before Wiggins and Smythe return."

But there wasn't anything to do except go about their normal routine. Betsy went upstairs to finish polishing the furniture, Mrs. Goodge mixed up her suet, and Mrs. Jeffries went upstairs to check the linen cupboard. But all of them worked just a bit faster than usual and with their ears cocked toward the door. They wanted to be at the ready, as it were, when the males of the household returned.

The rest of the morning seemed to crawl by at a snail's pace. Mrs. Jeffries replenished the supply of dewberry-wood chips and counted out the week's linen supply. She laid the sheets, towels, and cleaning rags on the table outside the cupboard, then withdrew to her quarters to finish the household accounts.

She entered her rooms and kept the door open so that she could hear when someone arrived back with news. Sitting down at her desk, she drew the account book out of the top drawer, opened it, and diligently picked up the stack of receipts sitting underneath the brass angel paperweight. The greengrocer's bill was on the top. She picked it up, studied the items on the list, and then dropped it onto the ledge. This was utterly pointless. She simply couldn't concentrate. Her mind was already too occupied with that strange tale the girl had told them. She knew it was because investigating murder — or in this case, attempted murder — had become virtually second nature to all of them. The housekeeper smiled to herself. Even Smythe and Betsy, who'd just recently become engaged, had postponed getting married because they were afraid they'd have to give up their snooping. They hadn't come right out and admitted that this was behind their reluctance to set a wedding date, but Mrs. Jeffries was fairly certain. Once Smythe and Betsy were married, they'd no doubt want their own house and their own life. A life certainly far grander than the one they lived now. Smythe, despite his efforts to keep his circumstances a secret, was a wealthy man. None of the others in the household, save for herself and Betsy, knew about the coachman's fortune.

She picked up the greengrocer's bill and put it back under the paperweight. She reflected for a moment on the strange circumstances that had led them all to the household of Gerald Witherspoon. She'd been a policeman's widow from York who'd decided to come to London because she was bored. She'd quite deliberately found a position as housekeeper to a policeman. The inspector had been happily working in the records room, but once she'd gotten him investigating and then solving those horrible Kensington High Street killings, well, everything had fallen into place rather neatly.

Smythe and Wiggins were already here when the inspector and she had arrived. They'd worked for Witherspoon's late aunt Euphemia. The inspector, though he had very little use for either a footman or a coachman, kept them both on. He'd not only inherited this house from his aunt, he'd also inherited a substantial fortune. Mrs. Goodge had come along a few weeks later, and then one night, Betsy, half-starved and looking like death was dogging her very footsteps, ended up on the inspector's door stoop. Gerald Witherspoon, being the man he was, insisted on taking the girl in, feeding her, and then giving her a position as maid.

That was the beginning. Now they were family. And they loved to snoop. Not that their dear inspector ever realized he was getting help from his own household on his cases. He didn't. Occasionally, though, others did.

She was shaken from her reverie by the sound of the front door shutting downstairs. Someone was back. She leapt up and fairly flew down the front stairs.

"Oh, Inspector —" She caught herself and slowed down when she reached the landing on the first floor. Recovering her poise, she continued down the stairs at her normal pace. "I didn't think you'd be home so early. Is everything all right?"

"Quite all right, Mrs. Jeffries." Witherspoon took off his hat and moved toward the new brass coatrack he'd recently bought. "Chief Inspector Barrows is having a dinner party tonight."

"A dinner party, sir?" Mrs. Jeffries beat him to the coatrack by a couple of seconds. She extended her arm, took the inspector's bowler, and placed it on the top.

Gerald Witherspoon was a middle-aged man with a mustache and thinning dark hair. His complexion was light and his features sharp and rather fine-boned. Behind a pair of wire-rim spectacles, he had kindly hazel eyes. He frowned in confusion at his housekeeper. "Apparently I'm invited to this dinner party. But I don't recall receiving an invitation. Do you remember our receiving one?"

"No, sir, I don't. Was the chief inspector absolutely certain he'd sent the invitation?"

"That was the awful part, Mrs. Jeffries, I couldn't ask." He started toward the back stairs. "You see, I wasn't really paying attention to the conversation, when all of a sudden Inspector Nivens poked me in the ribs and asked what I was going to bring Mrs. Barrows for her birthday. It was most awkward. At that very moment the chief inspector turned and looked in our direction. He told me not to be late tonight, otherwise he'd be stuck talking to his wife's brother. It was obvious that a celebration was planned and that I'd been invited."

"Oh dear, that *is* awkward. Excuse me, sir." She was practically running to keep up with him. "But if you'd like a cup of tea, I'll be happy to bring it to the drawing room." Drat, she didn't want the inspector hanging about the kitchen when they were beginning an investigation. It would be just their bad luck to have Wiggins come flying through the back door talking up a blue streak about the case.

Witherspoon reached the top of the back stairs and started down. "I shall require far more than a cup of tea," he called over his shoulder. "I shall require the good graces of you dear ladies."

"Good graces?" she repeated. She charged down the back stairs behind him. "Whatever does that mean, sir?"

"It means I shall need your help." He reached the bottom step. "We've not much time."

Mrs. Goodge and Betsy glanced up from the table as the inspector and Mrs. Jeffries entered. Both of them, to their credit, managed to quickly mask their surprise. "This is a nice treat, sir," the cook said heartily. "Have you come home to have tea with us?" He sometimes did have tea with them, though usually that was on Sundays.

"I've come home to throw myself on your mercy," he said, pulling out the chair at the head of the table. "I'm in a bit of a muddle. I've been invited to Chief Inspector Barrows's dinner party tonight. It's his wife's birthday, so I must take a present, you see."

The women all stared at him blankly. It was so quiet they could hear the clip-clop of horses' hooves on the street outside.

"You've plenty of time to buy a present, sir," Betsy finally said. "It's not even three o'clock yet. The shops are open for another three hours."

"Yes, yes, I'm aware of that. But I've no idea what on earth to buy the woman. That's why I nipped home, you see. I was hoping one of you might suggest the proper sort of present one should buy for a superior's spouse."

The women cast quick, covert glances at one another. They understood their inspector's dilemma; this was, indeed, a very delicate matter. But they had a dilemma of their own they considered equally important — namely, to get Inspector Witherspoon out of their kitchen before Smythe or Wiggins came barging in.

Mrs. Goodge took the initiative. "It's quite simple, sir. You must buy her something nice, but not too personal."

Witherspoon shook his head eagerly. "That's what I thought, too. I was thinking perhaps I ought to get her a nice carpetbag."

"Oh, that's too expensive, sir," Mrs. Jeffries said quickly. Witherspoon's face fell. "You don't want to get her a gift that will be nicer than the one her husband gives her."

"How about a box of lace runners?" the cook suggested. "They've got some lovely ones at Hunts on the Kensington High Street."

"That's a wonderful idea," Mrs. Jeffries agreed. She didn't really care what the inspector bought Chief Inspector Barrows's wife; she simply wanted him out of the kitchen. "It's a perfect gift for Mrs. Barrows. One can never have enough lace runners."

The inspector brightened. "Good, then I'll get them. I'm so glad I came home; I'd have never thought of something like that. I was thinking I ought to buy her some gloves."

"You've got be careful buying things to wear, sir," Betsy said quickly. "Some women are real particular about what they like and what they don't like."

Witherspoon looked at the carriage clock on the pine sideboard. He got to his feet. "I ought to have plenty of time to nip out and get the present. Uh, what color do you think I ought to get?"

"They only come in white or cream," Mrs. Goodge replied. "Either will do."

"Excellent, excellent. Well, thank you, ladies, you've been enormously helpful." He turned toward the back door as it banged open and the sound of running footsteps could be heard. A moment later, Wiggins, closely followed by a panting Fred, the household dog, came bounding into the kitchen.

Upon seeing the inspector, Fred charged across the floor and began bouncing up and down enthusiastically.

"Hello, old boy." Witherspoon was devoted to the bundle of brown-and-black fur. If the truth were known, he was just a tad jealous of the relationship that Wiggins and the dog shared.

"Cor blimey, sir, we didn't expect to see you," Wiggins looked curiously at the others as the inspector and Fred indulged in their mutual admiration.

Mrs. Jeffries smiled briefly and then explained why the inspector had come home.

"The ladies have been most helpful," Witherspoon exclaimed as he gave the dog one last pat. "Most helpful indeed. I shall be home as soon as I've made my purchase. The chief inspector lives in St. John's Wood, so I shall be needing the carriage tonight. Do be so kind as to let Smythe know." He was unable to resist giving the dog another stroke.

"We'll do that, sir." Mrs. Jeffries edged toward the hall, she wanted to get the man out of the house. Smythe wouldn't have much time to give his report if he had to go to the livery stable and get the carriage ready.

The inspector finally said his goodbyes

and, accompanied by Mrs. Jeffries, was soon heading toward the front door.

"What'll we do now?" Wiggins asked. He plopped down at the table and scratched the dog behind the ears. "Smythe's not gonna be pleased with 'avin' to cart the inspector around all evenin' on the first day of an investigation."

"It doesn't matter," Mrs. Goodge said. "We'll not be doing much tonight."

"We could 'ave a meeting with Luty and Hatchet," Wiggins suggested. "I think we'll want them to know what's goin' on."

Betsy shrugged. "It won't hurt Smythe to wait until tomorrow." She was secretly rather pleased that her beloved would spend the first night of the investigation driving the coach and not snooping about or shadowing that maid Martha. On several of their other murders, he'd been able to go out in the night and begin investigating while she and the other women had had to wait until the following day. For once, she might actually get the jump on him.

"Smythe's not goin' to like that." Wiggins grinned. "Especially after you 'ear what I found out down at the station. Constable Griffiths knew ever so much."

Just then Smythe came into the kitchen. "What am I not goin' to like?" he asked.

Chapter 2

Smythe wasn't pleased when he heard about the inspector's plans for the evening. "Bloomin' Ada," he muttered. "Why tonight? I wanted to talk to a few of my sources." Frowning, he plunked himself down at the table.

Mrs. Jeffries came back to the kitchen and took the chair the inspector had vacated only moments earlier. She turned to Wiggins. "I take it you believe Martha is telling the truth?"

"I 'ad a nice natter with Constable Griffiths," Wiggins replied. "That bloodhound did dig up a corpse. It was in the newspapers. But I guess none of us seen it."

"That's odd," Mrs. Jeffries murmured. "I generally make a note of things like bodies being found."

"He'd been murdered?" Mrs. Goodge prodded. Simply finding a body didn't guarantee one also found a murder.

"Throat was sliced like a butchered pig," the footman said cheerfully. "They don't 'ave a clue who done it, either. Like Martha said, he was a pickpocket. But Tim Porter wasn't much of anythin' else, if you know what I mean."

"Even petty thieves 'ave enemies," Smythe said.

"Yeah, but accordin' to Constable Griffiths, this bloke were known to avoid anythin' that was violent. Bit of a coward, so to speak."

The housekeeper nodded approvingly at the footman. "You've done very well. Did the constable share anything else with you?"

"You're not goin' to like this part." Wiggins's grin faded. "The case was given to Inspector Nivens on account of the victim bein' a known thief. No one expects he'll ever catch the killer. I'd bet against it myself."

"Indeed, that murderer has little to worry about, then," Mrs. Goodge snorted in derision. "Not if Nivens is on the hunt."

"Nivens couldn't find the back end of horse, not even if he was ridin' on it," Smythe muttered. "Let alone a murderer."

"They must not want to catch the killer." Betsy shook her head in disgust.

Mrs. Jeffries didn't try to stem the tide of anger directed at Inspector Nigel

Nivens. He was an ambitious, self-serving little toad who was always trying to prove that Witherspoon had help in solving his cases. He went tattling to the chief inspector at the slightest pretext and used a system of informants to solve what few burglary cases he had each year. He was the sort of fellow you didn't want to sit next to on a long train trip. Nigel Nivens's favorite topic was Nigel Nivens. Mrs. Jeffries loathed him. And she suspected that the feeling was mutual. On more than one occasion, she'd had to dodge both him and his questions. "Well, let's hope that this case doesn't involve Nivens more than necessary. We don't want him interfering with our investigation. Anything else, Wiggins?"

The footman frowned thoughtfully. He didn't want to leave something out. "Not that I can remember. I 'ad to be right careful when I was askin' questions." He grinned at Betsy. "Wouldn't want the constable to get suspicious."

"Can I tell my bit now?" Smythe asked. There was only the barest hint of impatience in his tone.

"By all means," the housekeeper replied.

"I followed Martha to Orley Road. As she got to the front door, it opened and this tall woman poked her head out and started natterin' at the girl."

"The maid used the front door?" Mrs. Goodge's voice was only the smallest bit disapproving. Which actually showed how far she'd come since she'd begun investigating with the others. When they'd first come together, the cook would have been of the opinion that there were no circumstances which would justify a servant using the front door. Under the influence of Mrs. Jeffries and the rest of them, however, she'd lost much of her snobbish attitude. Indeed, there were moments when she was almost radical in her views.

Smythe nodded.

"Could you hear what she said?" Betsy asked.

"I was too far away. But I'll tell ya one thing, that woman looked mighty worried."

"Then what happened?" Mrs. Jeffries asked. She wanted to hurry him along. There might be things that needed doing before the inspector returned.

"I waited a few minutes and then I nipped around the corner so that I could see the back of the house. The school's deserted, all right. Place looks like it's falling down."

"Did you go inside?" Mrs. Jeffries was

fairly certain she knew the answer already.

"Popped over the fence in two shakes of a lamb's tail. The caretaker weren't in sight, so I snooped about and had a good look at the wall dividing the school from the houses along Orley Road. There was two big indentions right there in the mud where a ladder'd been propped. You could still see 'em, and most importantly, there were a bunch of bricks missing from the top of the wall."

"What about the table?" Betsy asked. "If the wall is as high as Martha said it was, were you able to see where the table was?"

"I managed." He grinned at the maid. "I'm not a young'un, but no ten-foot wall will stop me from 'avin' a look. The table was pushed back away from the wall, but you could see by the scratch marks on the paving where it'd been. Any bricks dropping from the top could have clomped someone sitting there. Probably killed 'em, too."

"It still seems a very unreliable way to try and murder someone," Mrs. Jeffries mused.

"Maybe the killer's a stupid git," Wiggins suggested. "Not all murderers are smart —"

"We don't know that we have a murderer," the housekeeper interrupted. "All we know for certain is that Miss Gentry appears to be having some very unfortunate accidents." But she did know that they had a case; she could feel it in her bones.

"Three accidents in two weeks," the cook said. "That's an awful lot of bad luck if you ask me."

"What do we do now?" Betsy asked.

Everyone stared at Mrs. Jeffries. She thought about it for a moment and then said, "If all of you agree, I think we ought to proceed as we usually do."

There was a collective rumble of agreement.

"Should I go get Luty and Hatchet?" Wiggins asked. He started to get up but Mrs. Jeffries waved him back to his seat.

"That's a good idea," she said, "but do wait until after the inspector comes home. He may want to take Fred for a walk or something before he goes out. Besides, you've got to shine his good shoes and brush his dinner jacket."

Wiggins slumped back into his chair. "Can't someone else do that? I hate brushin' that jacket; all them little dusty bits go up my nose."

"There wouldn't be any dusty bits if you

44

kept the inspector's closet aired properly," Mrs. Goodge retorted.

As the household really didn't need a footman, Mrs. Jeffries had assigned Wiggins some light valet duties. Not that their employer expected such service, but only to keep the lad busy.

"What are you complainin' about?" Smythe said. "I'm stuck drivin' him to a dinner party this evening instead of feelin' out my sources. Someone might have known something about our Miss Gentry's troubles. Count yourself lucky, lad."

Smythe glanced mournfully at Betsy. She smiled back at him. They both knew that when he came home with the inspector tonight, Betsy would have a cup of hot tea waiting for him. If the housekeeper and the cook were safely asleep, she'd have a kiss waiting for him as well.

"I think you could put that time to good use," Wiggins said.

Smythe cocked an eyebrow at the youth. "Do ya now?"

"If it's a party, they'll be lots of people comin' in hansoms and private carriages. Seems to me you could ask about and talk to some of the cabbies, see if anyone knows anything about that carriage accident."

"Fat chance, lad." Smythe laughed.

"That 'appened over two weeks ago. The trail's gone cold, unless it were a paid job, and if that's the case, whoever did it ain't goin' to be talkin' about it in front of a bunch of cabbies."

"Besides, of all the things that have happened to Miss Gentry," Mrs. Jeffries added, "the incident with the carriage really could have been an accident. There are an awful lot of careless drivers about. But it was a rather good suggestion, Wiggins." She smiled kindly at the boy.

"Will you be going on your own to see Miss Gentry tomorrow?" the cook asked the housekeeper.

"No. If the rest of you are agreeable," Mrs. Jeffries replied, "I thought Betsy and I both should go. Two heads are better than one, you know. And while one of us is asking questions, the other can be keeping a sharp eye out. One never knows what one can learn by being observant."

Orley Road was a short row of two-story red-brick houses with small, enclosed front gardens. The entire street was sandwiched between open fields on one side and the deserted school on the other.

Betsy and Mrs. Jeffries were at number 17 Orley Road at exactly ten o'clock the next morning. The small brass knocker had just banged against the wood when Martha threw open the door. "I'm ever so glad to see you," she said brightly. "I was afraid you might change your mind about comin'."

"We wouldn't have done that," Betsy assured her.

"Of course not," Mrs. Jeffries confirmed.

"Come in, then. Miss Gentry is all ready for you. She's in the drawing room."

Mrs. Jeffries and Betsy stepped inside. From the small entryway, a flight of stairs curved up sharply to the second floor. Martha led them down a short, carpeted hallway and into a bright, airy sitting room. Sunlight streamed in through the lace curtains, the walls were a pale yellow, and there was a green-and-gold carpet on the floor.

A tall woman with a nice smile and lovely blue eyes got up from a cream-and-rose chintz settee as the women entered. "Mrs. Jeffries? I'm Annabeth Gentry. Thank you so much for coming."

"We hope we'll be able to help you," the housekeeper replied. She judged the woman to be about thirty-five or forty. She introduced Betsy and the two of them sat down. Betsy had a quick look around. The

47

room was nicely furnished but not cluttered. Two potted plants, a couple of nice pictures, an ottoman in the same shade of rose as the chair she was sitting on, and a matching set of bookcases on either side of the small fireplace.

"Martha told me all about you," Annabeth Gentry said as she resumed her seat, then turned her head toward the door. "Come in, Miranda; as you can see, we have visitors."

Betsy and Mrs. Jeffries both turned to look. A huge russet-colored bloodhound with a mournful face and enormously long ears loped into the room.

"What a lovely dog," Betsy exclaimed in delight. "So you're Miranda?"

The dog's tail wagged as she trotted over to give Betsy's outstretched hand a sniff. Betsy giggled and started petting the animal's shiny coat. "Oh, you're lovely, aren't you."

"She loves the attention." Annabeth laughed. The dog trotted over to her mistress and rubbed her big head against her knees. "That's right, she's my Miranda girl. She's just a bit spoiled, but she's so good-natured, I don't see any harm in it."

"She's the one that found the body?" Mrs. Jeffries asked gently, trying to get the investigation started.

"That's right. We were out taking a walk on those open fields off Loftus Road. I don't know if you know the area, but it's quite lovely. As there wasn't anyone about, I'd taken Miranda off the lead so she could have a bit of a run. All of a sudden she started sniffing the ground in that concentrated way she has and following it along the edge of the footpath for a good fifty feet. Then, just as suddenly, she turned sharply and stopped just inside a wooded area. She started digging frantically. When I saw the man's hand, I almost fainted. I called her away and went and got a policeman."

"Very wise of you, I'm sure." Mrs. Jeffries nodded. "And it was just after you and Miranda found that body that the attempts on your life began?"

"I really don't see how that poor man could be connected to what's happening to me." Annabeth sighed. "After the police arrived, I wasn't involved at all. They hustled me away very quickly. But I'm so confused now, I don't really know what to think. At first I thought I was just having a run of bad luck; it's not unheard of for horses to bolt. Then I was even willing to think that perhaps I was becoming accident-prone when those bricks started flying off the top of the wall; after all, it's an old wall. But when Miranda almost died from eating that poisoned cream, I knew for certain someone was really trying to kill me. You see, I was the one that should have eaten the cream. Not my poor hound."

"Tell us how this poisoning attempt took place," Betsy urged.

"I'm not sure I understand what you mean." Annabeth cocked her head to one side.

"We do need a few more details, Miss Gentry," Mrs. Jeffries explained. "Exactly when did it happen? Who was in the house? Where did the cream come from and how much of it had you consumed before Miranda helped herself?"

"Oh dear." She smiled apologetically. "I must sound as if I'm a dolt. Of course you need details. Let me see . . . well, it was the day before yesterday. My sister and her husband were visiting, so we were going to have tea outside. None of us particularly care for cream, but as we were having scones, Martha put it out along with the strawberry jam."

"Where did the cream come from?" Mrs. Jeffries asked. "I mean, why did you have it in the house if none of you care for it?"

"That's the strangest thing," Annabeth answered. "We don't know where it came from. But we didn't know we didn't know until after poor Miranda almost died from eating the wretched stuff, if you see what I mean. You see, when Martha went into the kitchen after searching for the curd, she saw a pot of cream on the table. Things have been a bit chaotic recently, what with getting ready for the move and all, so she naturally assumed I'd remembered we needed something for tea and purchased the cream. So she put it on the serving tray and brought it outside. When I saw the cream on the tray, I simply assumed that she'd nipped out and bought it herself. You see? Neither of us had actually bought the stuff, it was just here. But the circumstances were such that we didn't ask one another anything until after Miranda got ill."

Betsy thought she understood what the woman was saying. She glanced at Mrs. Jeffries. The housekeeper's expression revealed nothing. "Are you saying this pot of clotted cream just suddenly appeared on your kitchen table? Someone must have put it there."

"It makes no sense at all," Annabeth said

eagerly. "That's what's so baffling to us, too."

Mrs. Jeffries looked at the huge hound, who was now lying at her mistress's feet. "Miranda doesn't seem to have been harmed by the experience."

"Only because she'd just eaten a mouthful of the stuff," Annabeth said. "I'd put a very small amount on my scone and then I'd cut it up into pieces. Just at that time, my sister and her husband arrived and I got up to go greet them. Miranda, naughty girl that she is, stretched up and grabbed one of the pieces of scone. Then Bruce, that's Mrs. Aylesworthy's cat, bounded into the yard and Miranda took off after him. A few minutes later, just as we were sitting down for tea, Miranda came slinking back. The poor darling was retching terribly. I didn't know what was the matter. I asked Martha if Miranda had eaten anything —"

"And I said all she'd had since her breakfast was that bit of scone," Martha added.

"How did you know for certain it was the cream?" Betsy asked. "Couldn't it have been the scones?"

"No, my brother-in-law and my sister both ate the scones and they didn't have cream, so I realized that whatever had made Miranda ill had been in the cream. By then I realized Miranda had been poisoned," Annabeth said. "I'm rather an expert on dogs, you see. I don't have any formal medical training, but I know enough to spot the symptoms of poisoning. As soon as I got rid of my relatives, I gave Miranda a thorough examination and then I sent Martha into the larder for the cream. We were going to take it to the police. But it had vanished."

"Who was in the house that day?" Betsy asked. She thought that was a reasonable place to start.

Annabeth's expression grew thoughtful. Absently, she reached down and petted the huge dog. "Well, let's see, there was Martha and myself, of course. My sister and her husband were here for tea . . . well, they were here for part of the tea; after Miranda retched all over the terrace, they took themselves off fairly quickly."

"What are their names?" Mrs. Jeffries asked.

"Reverend and Mrs. Cooksey." Annabeth grinned. "That's how they insist on introducing themselves. I always think of them as Harold and Louisa, but that tends to annoy them. Then my other sister and her husband popped in later that day. They're Elliot and Ethel Caraway. They'd stopped by to see how the renovations on the new house were going."

"Anyone else?"

"My new neighbor, Mr. Eddington; he came around to bring me the name of his painters. Oh, there were ever so many people here that day. I expect that's one of the reasons we didn't pay much attention to that wretched cream."

Betsy's head was spinning. She had dozens of questions to ask. From the expression on Mrs. Jeffries's face, she was certain the housekeeper had quite a few as well. "I know what you mean; some days there's so much coming and going you don't know what's what."

"Miss Gentry." Mrs. Jeffries smiled. "Let's put the issue of how the cream got into the house to one side. I've a few more things to ask, if you don't mind."

"But of course you do." Annabeth nodded vigorously. "That's why you've come. To help me. I must say, I'm ever so grateful. I don't think anyone else would take me seriously. Why, even my own sister didn't believe me."

"We believe you," Betsy said. "But like Mrs. Jeffries said, before we can do you any good at all, we'll have to ask you a lot of questions."

Martha started for the kitchen. "I'll get the kettle on. We'll all think better over a cup of tea."

Wiggins hoped that Mrs. Jeffries wouldn't get angry when she found out what he'd done, but he didn't fancy sitting around the kitchen with Mrs. Goodge, waiting for the others to get back. He stopped in front of the gate of what had been Helmsley's Grammar School for Boys and peeked through the rusted iron railings into the yard. The building was three stories tall and made of brick. Several of the top windows were broken and the eaves over the attic were missing bits of masonry. The aged gray-red cobblestones in the wide courtyard were split in spots and patches of grass pushed up between the cracks.

Wiggins sighed in disappointment. He wasn't sure what he expected to find here. Smythe had already had a good look about the place. "We might as well see what's what, Fred." He glanced at the animal standing patiently at his heels. Fred pricked his ears and woofed gently in agreement. "It looks deserted. But you never know, we might stumble onto something important."

He put his foot on the bottom rail of the gate and started to hoist himself up. The latch popped and the gate squeaked open. Fred trotted through, turned, and woofed at Wiggins, who was having a difficult time getting his foot out from between the railings. " 'Ang on a minute," he told the dog. Not one to waste a lot of energy, Fred promptly sat down. Wiggins extricated his foot and squeezed through the opening.

To his left, the courtyard narrowed and wound to the back of the school. Two small, dilapidated sheds were on the far side and behind them was the wall which separated the school grounds from the neighboring houses. Wiggins glanced to his right; there was a high wall on the far side of the school building, and over it, he could see the spires of a church.

"Come on, Fred, let's have a look-see down by them buildings." He and Fred headed across the cobblestones. In the quiet morning, the heels of his heavy work shoes seemed horribly loud. He could even hear the click of Fred's nails against the stones. He stopped in front of the first building but it didn't look very interesting, so he continued on to the next. "This seems as good a place as any," he said to the dog. "Let's go 'round the back and see if we can spot them ladder marks in the dirt."

But Fred wasn't listening to Wiggins, he was staring at the shed they'd just passed. The hair on his back stood up and his ears had gone back. He was rooted to the spot.

A shiver of fear snaked up Wiggins's spine. They were now out of sight of the street and he suddenly felt very alone. He knelt down close to the dog's ear. "What is it, boy? What's wrong?" he whispered.

Not taking his gaze off the shed, Fred began to growl.

"Maybe we'd best get out of here," Wiggins said. He began rising to his feet and backing away. "Come on, boy, let's go."

But the dog didn't budge. His growl turned into a snarl.

From the inside of the shed, there was a loud, metallic thump.

Wiggins was no coward, but he knew in his bones that he and Fred had to get out of there. He didn't know how he knew it; he simply knew that if they didn't go now, something horrible would happen. He turned and started for the gate. "Come on, Fred," he hissed, "let's go."

Fred began to bark.

There was another frightening thump from the shed and then a loud whack as something banged against the door.

Wiggins reached down, picked up the dog, tucked him under his arm, and ran for the gate. Surprised, Fred stopped barking. He started up again a moment later, but by then, Wiggins had pushed the dog through the opening and was shimmying through himself. Wiggins heard the shed door opening. He knew he ought to look around, to get a look at whoever was behind him, but for the life of him, he was too scared.

Still barking, Fred tried to run back through the gate. Wiggins grabbed his collar and dragged him back. "Come on, boy," he called, frantically trying to keep the animal under control, "let's run. Come on, let's 'ave us a good run." Praying his tactic would work, he let go the collar and ran across the empty road. For a fraction of a second, Fred hesitated, then he took off after his beloved friend.

They ran down around the corner and onto Frithville Gardens and then onto the Uxbridge Road. Wiggins didn't stop till he and Fred were in sight of the railway lines and surrounded by people. He skidded to a halt when he reached the Albion Brewery and slumped against the side of the building. Sweat poured down his face as he took in huge gulps of air. He could feel the rough brick through his thin shirt. "Good dog." He reached down and petted the panting Fred. "You followed my lead. It's not that I'm a coward, Fred, but there was somethin' evil back there. I could feel it in me bones."

Fred woofed softly and wagged his tail.

"Now we've got to suss out what to do next," Wiggins said. He often talked to Fred. The fact that he was on a busy London street and that several passerbys were staring at him oddly didn't bother him in the least. "Someone's got to go back to that place." He started toward Shepherd's Bush Green. "I know there's somethin' wrong. But I'll have a devil of a time convincin' anyone to 'ave a look-see in that shed. What can I tell 'em? That I 'eard some funny noises? They'll wonder why I didn't 'ave a look myself." He stopped by a street lamp to let a handsome brougham pulled by two elegant gray horses go past. Wiggins knew that no one at Upper Edmonton Gardens would make fun of him for running away, nor would anyone consider him a coward. In truth, they'd probably tell him he'd acted wisely. But now that he was safely away from that place, he felt silly.

But he didn't feel silly enough to go back to that shed alone. Not by himself.

A costermonger pushing a creaky cart trundled past, leaving the pungent scent of mussels and jellied eels in its wake. Wiggins sighed and started across the road. "There's nothing for it, Fred," he said to the dog. "There's only one thing to do now. We've got to find Smythe."

"What do you think, Mrs. Jeffries?" Betsy asked as soon as they were out of earshot of the Gentry house.

"I think we'd best get everyone together and try to make some sense of all this," the housekeeper replied. They walked toward the omnibus stop at the top of the road. "But I've no doubt now that someone is trying to kill the woman."

"Should we involve the inspector?" Betsy stared up the road, her head bobbing from side to side as she tried to see if the omnibus was coming. But there was too much traffic to see much of anything.

"Not at this time," Mrs. Jeffries replied.

"Why?" Betsy looked at her curiously. "Don't you believe Miss Gentry?"

"Absolutely. But we've no proof. The poison cream disappeared and the other two incidents could both have been accidents. At least that's what the police will say. We need a bit more evidence before we involve the inspector. But I've no doubt we shall find it. Miss Gentry gave us plenty of information to begin our inquiry. Oh look, here comes the omnibus. When we get on, why don't you continue on to the Kensington High Street and Knightsbridge."

Betsy laughed. "So that's why you wanted us to take the omnibus instead of walking. You want me to get Luty and Hatchet."

"Of course, have them back at Upper Edmonton Gardens by teatime. We've much to discuss."

Betsy frowned. "Will Smythe be back by then? For that matter, did he say where he was going today?" He'd been very close-mouthed this morning and she, of course, had too much pride to pry. She wasn't going to become a nosy nellie simply because they'd got engaged. But she was just a tad hurt that he'd gone off without saying anything to her.

Mrs. Jeffries opened her coin purse and took out two ha'pennies and a sixpence. The omnibus pulled to a stop and the two women, holding tightly on to the wooden

61

handrail, climbed aboard. There were two seats just inside. Mrs. Jeffries slid in by the window, leaving Betsy the one on the aisle. She handed the coins to the conductor and said, "One for Holland Park Road and one for the Kensington High Street."

Smythe wasn't in a good mood. He hung the harness on to the wall of the tack room and stepped into the stable proper. Howards, the livery where the inspector stabled his horses and carriage, was a large commercial concern, but at this time of day, it was relatively quiet.

He pulled the door shut behind him, locked it, and walked across the aisle to the stall where Bow and Arrow munched happily on their fresh oats. "Bloomin' Ada," he muttered to himself, "it's been a waste of a day. That's what I get for tryin' to be clever. A bleedin' wild goose chase."

"What kind of wild goose chase?" Wiggins asked as he and Fred popped around the corner and into view.

Surprised, Smythe started and then quickly caught himself. "What the blazes are you doin' 'ere?"

"I come to find you." Wiggins grinned. "I didn't know ya talked to yourself."

"I don't."

"Then who was ya talkin' to? The horses?"

"All right, every once in a while I talk to myself. What of it? Why was ya lookin' for me? Did Mrs. Jeffries send ya?"

Wiggins's smile faded. He looked down at the dog, who'd plopped down by his feet. "Uh, I need some 'elp with something."

"What are you on about, lad?" Smythe asked. He looked carefully at the boy; a line of sweat clung to his hairline and his face was flushed. Fred was panting like he'd run with the hounds of hell on his heels. "And let's get that dog some water. Fred's tongue's hangin' out."

They made their way to the pump in the front of the stable. The scent of horse and manure wasn't as strong out in the open air. Wiggins worked the handle and water gushed into the trough. Fred helped himself.

"Now, what's all this about, then?" Smythe asked softly. He could tell by the boy's expression that something serious was clouding his mind.

"You've got to promise not to laugh at me," Wiggins muttered. He kept his gaze on Fred.

" 'Ave I ever laughed at you?"

Wiggins shook his head. "It's just that this sounds so silly, but it's not. It were real. I felt it. Something 'appened there. Somethin' awful. Fred felt it, too."

Smythe was genuinely alarmed now. Wiggins could go a bit foolish over a pretty lass, but he had good instincts. Alarmed, his voice was harsher than he intended. "What are you talkin' about? What's wrong?"

"I went over to that school you was at yesterday," Wiggins began. "The one next to that Miss Gentry's house."

"Why? I'd already had a good gander about the place, already said them bricks 'ad been pried off the top and pushed over the wall. What was you hopin' to find?"

Wiggins shrugged. "I'm not sure. But it wasn't like I 'ad anythin' else to do, so I went along and 'ad a look myself. Fred and I squeezed through the gate and we was just startin' down that bend toward the back when Fred stopped dead in his tracks and we 'eard somethin' comin' from the second shed."

"What do you mean, you 'eard somethin'? What'd ya 'ear?"

"I don't know what it was," Wiggins admitted. "But it scared me. Scared Fred, too. His hackles come up and his ears went

64

back and then 'e started barkin' —"

"Well, what was it?"

"I don't know." Wiggins slumped his shoulders. "I got so scared I ran. I picked Fred up and ran like the devil. That's why I come 'ere to get you. I know somethin' bad was in that shed and I want you to come back with me."

Betsy arrived back at Upper Edmonton Gardens a few minutes before tea. Luty Belle Crookshank and her butler, Hatchet, accompanied her.

"We got here as quick as we could," Luty exclaimed. She was a small, thin elderly American woman with white hair, brown eyes so dark they looked almost black, and a razor-sharp mind. She loved bright clothes almost as much as she loved investigating crime. This afternoon she wore a huge hat decorated with yellow flowers and two bright purple plumes, a lavender dress with lace on the collars and cuffs, and a pair of outrageously huge amethyst earrings.

"Good day, everyone," Hatchet said politely as he followed Luty into the kitchen. "I hope all is well with the household." He was a tall man in his late fifties, with a full head of snow-white hair, a dignified de-

65

meanor, and a love of detective work that surpassed even his employer's.

"We are all well," Mrs. Jeffries replied. She nodded toward the others. "Do sit down and have some tea. We're just waiting for Wiggins and Smythe to come before we begin. They ought to be here any moment now." She looked at the maid. "What have you told them?"

"Just that Miss Gentry wants us to find out who is trying to kill her. That's all."

"Girl's lips were sealed tighter than a bank vault," Luty said. She took the empty seat next to the cook.

"To be fair, madam," Hatchet said as he slipped into the seat next to Mrs. Jeffries, "Miss Betsy explained that she wanted to wait until the others could be here to share what she and Mrs. Jeffries learned today."

"I wasn't trying to be mysterious," Betsy said earnestly. "I just didn't think Mrs. Jeffries would want us having to explain everything twice. Besides, Wiggins and Smythe'll be here soon. I'm sure of it. They know we were going to be having one of our meetings."

"Maybe we'd better leave Fred out 'ere," Wiggins suggested. "We could tie 'im to the inside of the gate."

66

"Why do that?" Smythe asked curiously. "Seems to me if you're right and there's somethin' amiss back at that shed, we'd do best to 'ave Fred with us."

Fred wagged his tail and woofed softly, as though he agreed with the coachman.

"Well, if ya think so, but he barked 'is 'ead off before." Wiggins started up the short drive to the gate.

"Wait a minute," Smythe ordered. "I thought you told me you run off like the 'ounds of 'ell was on yer 'eels?"

"I did."

"Then who closed the ruddy thing behind you?" Smythe asked.

Wiggins stared at the now-closed gate and shook his head. "I swear, it were open when I left. I was carryin' Fred and I didn't stop to pull it closed."

Smythe frowned at the latch. "It's not locked, just pulled up close together. This is gettin' interestin'." He edged the gate open and squeezed his big frame through.

Fred jumped through and Wiggins followed. Once they were all inside, Smythe stood for a moment. Cautiously, he looked to his left and then his right. Then he turned his attention to the derelict school building. His gaze started at the top and scanned the windows, assuring himself that none of the curtains moved or twitched. After he'd satisfied himself that they weren't being watched, he said, "Show me where you 'eard these noises at, then."

Wiggins started across the cobblestones. "It's just 'round there." Now that the moment was at hand, he hoped he wouldn't disgrace himself in front of the person he most admired. But as they headed for the shed, he found his steps slowing. Even Fred's frisky trot suddenly slowed to a much more sedate pace. He didn't like where this walk was heading.

From the corner of his eyes, Smythe saw Wiggins dropping behind. He knew then that the lad had really been frightened. But he didn't let that rattle him. Wiggins was a bit on the imaginative side. What did set the hair on the back of Smythe's neck prickling was when he noticed the dog's reaction. Cor blimey, he thought, what's going on here?

They reached the shed. Wiggins took a deep breath. Fred sniffed the crack under the door and whined softly. Smythe gave the door a gentle nudge. Slowly, it creaked open and a shaft of sunlight illuminated the dark space.

The inside of the place was covered with cobwebs and dust. A wooden bench with missing slats ran the length of the small room. In the dim light, it was hard to make out much detail, but Smythe could see where the dust on the stone floor had been disturbed.

"Do you see anything?" Wiggins asked.

"Just a lot of dirt and mess . . ." Smythe paused as he spotted a large mound on the far side of the room. He pushed the door open wide to get more light into the room. "Damn." He charged inside and flew over to the mound.

"What is it?" Wiggins cried as he followed quick on Smythe's heels. Fred whined softly, hesitated, and then charged inside.

"It's a man." Smythe knelt down beside the bench, pulled the body onto its back, and began feeling for a pulse. He yanked open the man's shirt collar and skimmed his fingers across the flesh, hoping to feel the spark of life.

"Is he dead?" Wiggins's heart sank to his toes. He knew the answer already. And it was probably his fault.

Smythe said nothing for a moment; then he sighed and sat back on his heels. " 'E's a goner, lad."

"Is there any blood?" Wiggins asked softly. He silently prayed that the man had

69

died of natural causes. But deep in his bones, he knew that probably wasn't the case.

"No." Smythe straightened the collar back into place and tried vainly to smooth out the fabric. "But then there wouldn't be. There's bruises all over 'is throat. I'm no expert, but unlessin' 'e strangled 'imself, someone's murdered the poor bloke."

Chapter 3

"What's keeping them?" Mrs. Goodge asked irritably. "They knew we were going to be having a meeting this afternoon."

"I'm sure they'll be here any moment," Mrs. Jeffries said soothingly. "Smythe was going to take the horses for a run; you know how busy the roads get in the afternoons. There's always delays of one sort or another."

"What about Wiggins?" Luty asked. "Where in the dickens is he?"

The housekeeper took a sip of tea. "No one seems to know where Wiggins has gone. Apparently, Fred's with him."

"You ought to speak to him about that," Mrs. Goodge said. "He oughtn't to go off on his own without telling one of us where he's going and when he'll be back. What if the inspector needed him?"

"I'm sure the lad has a good reason for being tardy," Hatchet interjected.

"He'd better," the cook murmured. She hated it when Wiggins disappeared like this. She wouldn't for the world let anyone know, but she did worry so about the boy. He did have his head in the clouds so much of the time and anything could happen if you weren't careful. "Left here this morning without so much as a by-your-leave."

They all turned as they heard the back door opening and the sound of rushing footsteps in the hall.

Smythe flew into the kitchen, followed closely by Wiggins and Fred. "We've got trouble," the coachman said without preamble.

"What kind of trouble?" Mrs. Jeffries asked.

"There's a dead man in the school behind Miss Gentry's 'ouse. Looks to me like 'e's been strangled."

"I take it you haven't sent for the police," she stated calmly.

Smythe shook his head. "Not yet. We wanted to 'ave a word with you lot first."

"You're quite sure the victim was murdered?" she asked.

"There's a ring around the feller's throat," Smythe reported grimly. "Looks like a garrote of some kind was used."

"Any idea who the man is?" Mrs. Goodge asked.

"We think it's the caretaker," Wiggins added.

"How do you know?" Hatchet asked.

"When we rolled 'im over, these come tumblin' out of 'is pocket." Wiggins pulled a brass ring with several keys hanging from it out of his trouser pocket. "The back door of the school was open, too. Stands to reason, doesn't it; the caretaker would be the one with keys."

"Strange that an abandoned building would have a caretaker," Luty muttered. "Are you sure he ain't just some tramp that wandered in off the street?"

"We're not sure of anythin' yet," Smythe said. "We're only guessin'. But right now who the feller was isn't our problem; figuring out what we're going to tell the police is. We'd no business bein' there and now we've got to think of a way to get the police to that body without lettin' 'em know it were Wiggins and I that found it."

"You must go right to the inspector," Mrs. Goodge insisted.

"And what would we say when 'e asks what we was doin' there in the first place?" Smythe returned archly.

"What *were* you doing there?" Mrs. Jeffries asked curiously.

Smythe hesitated and then looked at the

footman. Wiggins blushed a deep rosy color and looked at the dog sitting at his feet. "Smythe was there because I went and got 'im," he finally admitted. "I was there earlier, Mrs. Jeffries. I decided I'd nip along and 'ave a look while you was talkin' to Miss Gentry. I weren't followin' you or anythin' like that; I just thought I'd get a bit of jump on the case, so to speak."

"But Smythe had already been to the school and had a look around," Betsy pointed out.

"I know that," Wiggins explained. "But I didn't want to sit about 'ere waitin'. I was tryin' to 'elp."

"I'm sure you were, Wiggins," Mrs. Jeffries interjected. "Now, tell us how you came to find the body."

" 'E didn't exactly find it," Smythe said. " 'E 'eard some suspicious noises and, quite rightly, came along to 'Owards to get me."

"Suspicious noises?" Luty repeated. "What does that mean?"

" 'E 'eard a few thumps comin' from the shed," Smythe explained, "and then Fred started barkin' his fool 'ead off. So the lad did the smart thing and took off before anyone got suspicious and came out to see what all the ruckus was about. It didn't take 'im long; 'Owards is only about twenty minutes away. We went back to the school and had a look in the shed; that's when we found the bloke."

It was quite obvious that Smythe and Wiggins were giving only a bare-bones version of the story. Consequently, no one said anything. Finally, after the silence stretched to an embarrassing length, Mrs. Jeffries said, "It's always best to avoid making a spectacle of oneself, especially if one suspects something untoward is afoot. It was clever of you to dash off and get Smythe. Two heads are always better than one in a precarious situation. Now, why don't the two of you sit down, have a cup of tea, and we'll come up with a way to get our inspector out to that corpse."

Inspector Gerald Witherspoon pushed the heavy iron gate open. "Do you think we ought to have brought some more men along, Constable Barnes?"

Barnes, a tall man with a craggy face and a headful of iron-gray hair under his policeman's helmet, glanced over his shoulder at the two constables trailing them. "If there really is a body, sir, we've enough men to secure the area and send off for the police surgeon."

"Oh, I'm sure there's a body," Witherspoon said. "That's not the sort of thing that Wiggins would make a mistake about."

"What was the lad doing in this neighborhood?" Barnes asked curiously.

"He said he was looking for a haberdashery." The inspector stopped abruptly and stared at the forlorn brick building which had once been a school. Following his footman's instructions, he turned his gaze to where the cobblestones wound around the corner and spotted the two sheds. "My housekeeper thinks I need a new bowler. She sent Wiggins off to check the prices. I suppose it's in there." He pointed to the farther shed.

"I'll just have a quick look, sir." Knowing his superior was quite squeamish when it came to death, Barnes hurried on ahead. He opened the door and stuck his head inside. "It's here, sir. Just where young Wiggins said it would be."

Witherspoon took a long, deep breath. He knew his duty. He had to examine the body. "All right, Constable, let's have at it." Together, he and Barnes stepped inside.

"Your dog must have a good nose," Barnes commented as he stepped around the bench. "It's a good seventy yards from the road to this shed."

"Fred didn't actually smell anything from the road." He laughed nervously. "Wiggins said he was feeling quite frisky, and as there weren't many people about, he'd let him off the lead. Well, you know how dogs are, he started dashing about and slipped through the fence. The lad went after him, but by this time Fred must have had some sort of scent because he ran up to the shed, began howling his head off, and started scratching at the door. It swung open and Fred ran inside. Well, of course, Wiggins had no choice but to go after him." Witherspoon sighed. "Poor lad, it was quite dreadful for him. He seemed very upset when he came to the station to tell me what happened. That's one of the reasons I didn't want him to accompany us back here. He's not one of us, you know. He's not used to some of the awful things we must deal with."

"Yes, sir," Barnes agreed dryly. But he didn't share his superior's opinion of Wiggins. It seemed to him the lad was quite capable of dealing with a wide variety of police like activity. The boy had been in at the arrest often enough. For that matter, half the inspector's household sometimes seemed to show up at the very moment when a bit of assistance was most needed. But Barnes was careful not to share his suspicions about the activities of the inspector's servants. Especially not around the station. There were some that were jealous of Witherspoon's success in solving murders.

"We'd better get on with it." The inspector stifled a shudder as he looked at the dead man's face. "Poor fellow. What an ugly place to die." At least this one wasn't oozing blood everywhere.

Constable Barnes knelt down on the other side and examined the body. He saw the ligature mark around the throat right away. "It's a murder, sir. You'll have to have a gander. The man's been strangled."

Somehow, the inspector wasn't surprised. Every corpse he came in contact with turned out to be a murder victim. "I was rather hoping the fellow had died of heart failure or some other natural cause." He sighed. "Send one of the constables back to the station for the surgeon and an ambulance. We'll need more lads as well. We'd best search the school and the grounds. We'll need to do a house-to-house in the neighborhood as well." He knelt beside the body and took a quick peek at the marks on the fellow's throat. "Let's go through his clothes."

"Right, sir." Barnes opened the man's jacket and stuck his fingers in the inside pocket. "Nothing here, sir."

Witherspoon held his breath and stuck his hand into the man's trouser pocket. He pulled out two ha'pennies and a shilling.

"What about your lad, sir?" Barnes asked. He was rifling through the other pocket, looking for anything which would identify the fellow. "You'll have to speak to him again."

Witherspoon frowned. "Wiggins? Why?"

"He's a witness, sir," Barnes said calmly.

"But he's told us everything he knows." The inspector stood up. He decided they could finish examining the victim's clothing after the police surgeon arrived.

"He thinks he has, sir." Barnes rose to his feet as well. "But as you always say, sir, " 'People know more than they think they do.' That's one of the reasons you're so clever at catching killers. You're always digging for that extra bit of information."

"Ah yes." The inspector nodded vaguely. He wasn't sure he liked being reminded of all the things he'd said in the past. His housekeeper had a habit of doing the same thing. But then again, it was flattering to know that his constable listened when he spoke. But really, did he have to remember every single word? "Quite right. Much as I dislike upsetting the poor lad, I suppose we've no choice."

"What the dickens do we do now?" Luty demanded. "I don't want to waste any more time sittin' around this table. There's investigatin' to be done!"

"Patience, madam, patience," Hatchet said. "We can't investigate anything until we've decided what, precisely, it is we're to investigate."

"If you ask me, it's got to be the dead man," Mrs. Goodge said stoutly.

"But what about Miss Gentry, then?" Betsy asked. "Just because someone's been strangled, we can't ignore her problem. Someone is still trying to do her in."

"I think Miss Gentry's troubles must be related to the dead man," Hatchet interjected. "It would be a very big coincidence to have a murder and an attempted murder within a hundred yards of one another."

"I agree," Mrs. Jeffries said quickly. She was in a real quandary. On the one hand, it might be prudent to wait until after the inspector returned home this evening before they began their investigation, while on the other, she felt one should strike while the iron was hot. "And as at least one of the attempts on Miss Gentry appears to come from the school property, I think we can safely assume the incidents are related."

"Right, then." Smythe grinned widely. "Let's get crackin'."

"Before we do anything," Mrs. Jeffries said, "we need to discuss what we know. In the interests of logic, my suggestion is that we discuss the details that Miss Gentry gave us earlier today. Perhaps by then, Wiggins will have returned." She took a quick sip from her teacup.

"Do you think Miss Gentry might have killed this fellow?" Mrs. Goodge asked. "I mean, perhaps she found out he was the one trying to do her in and took matters into her own hands, so to say."

"That's possible, of course," the house-keeper said thoughtfully. "But I'm not sure it's likely. From what Wiggins told us, he heard noises in the shed at about the same time we were speaking with Miss Gentry."

"Now, just a fast minute here," Luty said. "You're forgettin' something. You haven't told Hatchet and me much of anything yet. Come on, tell us everything that's happened so far and don't be leavin' out any details."

"Oh dear, I *am* sorry. You're quite right. We have let things get out of hand a bit since you arrived." Mrs. Jeffries gave Luty and Hatchet a complete report. "So you see," she concluded, "we've got ourselves a very complicated case here."

"What did you find out from Miss Gentry this morning?" the cook asked. She needed names. Her methods of investigating depended on cajoling gossip out of visiting tradespeople and working a network of informants from one end of London to the other.

"We found out who benefits if Miss Gentry suddenly meets her Maker," Betsy announced. "And quite a few other things as well."

"What about the body her dog discovered?" Mrs. Goodge frowned. She already had that name, but one never knew what other name might pop up in connection with the pickpocket. "We mustn't forget him. He might have something to do with this mess."

"Miss Gentry had no dealings with Tim Porter before Miranda dug him up," Mrs. Jeffries said. "She claims she knows nothing about him. But we won't forget him. You're quite right, Porter may have more to do with this than meets the eye. Now, as

Betsy was saying, the first thing we did was to find out who gains in the event of Miss Gentry's death." Of the murders they'd investigated, money was by far the most common motive for killing.

"What does she have to leave? I thought you said she was a spinster lady who lived in a little house over on Orley Road," the cook said.

"Is she rich?" Luty asked bluntly. She was always one to get to the heart of the matter.

"She is now," Betsy replied. "Miss Gentry just inherited a huge house and a large fortune."

"And her relatives aren't precisely pleased by her new circumstances," Mrs. Jeffries added. "She's got two married sisters, both of whom have already let it be known that they feel a single lady shouldn't be in charge of such wealth. They're putting pressure on her to let one of their husbands oversee Miss Gentry's money. But she's not having it. She wants to do it herself."

"Who left her the goods?" Smythe asked.

Betsy laughed. "Her almost mother-in-law. A woman named Clara Dempsey. A few years back, Miss Gentry was engaged to Cecil Dempsey, Clara's son. He died, so they never married. Miss Gentry kept on seeing Mrs. Dempsey. The women were very close. Miss Gentry helped take care of Mrs. Dempsey in the last years of her life, when the poor old thing was ill. No one knew it, but Mrs. Dempsey was rich. When she died, she left her big house and a huge number of stocks and bonds to Miss Gentry."

"She had a big house but no one knew she was rich?" Luty looked skeptical.

"The house is very run-down. Miss Gentry's having a lot of work done to fix it up."

"I take it that Miss Gentry has been pressured to make a will?" Hatchet said.

"Oh yes." Mrs. Jeffries smiled cynically. "As soon as her sisters heard about her inheritance, they hustled her to a solicitor and got a will drawn up. One of the sisters is married to a barrister."

"I'll bet he was the one who recommended which solicitor Miss Gentry used," Smythe finished.

Mrs. Jeffries smiled knowingly. "I know, it's all so predictable. But that's one of the sad commentaries about life. People often *are* predictable, especially where money is concerned. Now, we've got to decide how we want to investigate this matter."

"If you'll give me the names of Miss

Gentry's relatives," Mrs. Goodge said, "I'll get cracking and see what my sources can find out. If one of them is a barrister, someone will know something."

"You oughta get an earful about him. No one ever says anything good about lawyers," Luty said. "I've got a pack of 'em working for me and there ain't a one of 'em I'd trust further than I could throw him."

"Really, madam." Hatchet sniffed disapprovingly. "Sir Oswald would be most offended to hear you speaking like that."

"Why don't we split the investigation in two?" Smythe suggested quickly. He didn't want anyone sidetracked by one of Luty and Hatchet's arguments, not this early in the game. "Wiggins and I can concentrate on finding out about the bloke that was strangled and the rest of you can concentrate on Miss Gentry."

No one said anything as they thought about his suggestion.

"I'm not sure that's a good idea," Mrs. Goodge finally murmured. "Surely the cases are connected."

Betsy looked doubtful. "I don't know, maybe we ought to do both at the same time."

"You're just scared you'll miss something," Smythe teased.

"It hasn't escaped my notice you're the one taking the actual murder," she shot back, "and leaving the rest of us to work on what might turn out to be a silly woman's imagination."

"I don't think so, Betsy," Mrs. Jeffries interjected. "As we discussed earlier, the cases have to be connected, and Smythe is right, we must have some way of going about our investigation in a way that won't leave us all confused."

Betsy didn't look convinced. "Oh, all right. I suppose it's the best we can do for now. But I'm reserving the right to poke my nose into the actual murder if it turns out Miss Gentry's making up tales."

"Me, too," Mrs. Goodge said. "Now, what's the name of Miss Gentry's two sisters and their husbands? I might as well get my sources sussin' out what's what."

"Ethel is married to Elliot Caraway. He's the barrister. They live in Kensington," Mrs. Jeffries explained. "The other sister is married to a vicar." She frowned. "Oh dear, I seem to have forgotten her name . . ."

"It's Louisa," Betsy said, "Louisa Cooksey. She's married to the Reverend Harold Cooksey. They live in Hammersmith, quite close to Miss Gentry."

"Where's his parish?" Hatchet asked.

"He doesn't have one," the housekeeper said. "Miss Gentry was a bit reticent about discussing her relatives. One can't blame her for that; it wouldn't be pleasant to think one's sister wanted you dead because you'd inherited a bit of money."

"And a house," Betsy reminded her.

"Where's the house at?" Luty asked.

"On the far side of the school, just beyond the church." Mrs. Jeffries took a sip of tea. "From what I gather, Mrs. Dempsey had lived there for many years. It needs quite a bit of repair. As I said, Miss Gentry is having a lot of work done, and apparently there's been a number of problems and delays in the past two weeks."

Luty nodded. "Fixing up an old house is always aggravating."

"If Miss Gentry spent a lot of time with her late fiancé's mother," Hatchet suggested, "perhaps I can ask about the neighborhood over there and see if there's anyone from her past with Mrs. Dempsey that wishes her harm."

Mrs. Jeffries stared at him in surprise. "Do you think that's worth your time?"

Hatchet hesitated. "I've no idea, but in many of our earlier investigations, it's

87

sometimes been the one place we didn't look that produced the murderer. Besides, with Mrs. Goodge working her sources for information on Miss Gentry's family, Miss Betsy asking around the current neighborhood, and Smythe and Wiggins finding out about our murder victim, there isn't much left for me to do at this point."

"What about me?" Luty demanded. "I need something."

"Of course you do, madam," Hatchet said smoothly. "But if I know you, you'll play the innocent while all along you've already decided to find out everything you can about everyone's bank balance." He only said this because he knew this was precisely what his employer had planned.

"Hmmph," Luty snorted. "You think you know me so well." In truth, she was planning on having a chat with her sources in the City early the following morning. She might as well get some use out of those old windbags who were watching her money. God knows they all liked to talk; they bent her ear often enough about what she should and shouldn't do with her own cash.

"Precisely, madam." Hatchet gave a satisfied smile.

"Are we going to wait for Wiggins?"

Mrs. Goodge glanced at the clock on the pine dresser. "It's getting late."

" 'E ought to be back 'ere anytime now," Smythe replied. "He's 'ad plenty of time to get down to the station, say 'is piece, and get back."

"What if he went with the inspector back to that shed?" Betsy said.

Smythe's smile disappeared. "Bloomin' Ada, I 'ope 'e's enough sense not to go back to that ruddy place. Poor lad felt bad enough —"

"I'm not surprised," Mrs. Goodge interrupted. "Finding a body isn't very pleasant, the lad'll be having nightmares if he's not careful."

"It wasn't just findin' the corpse that upset him —" Smythe broke off as they heard the back door open. Fred, who'd been having a nap at the coachman's feet, jumped up and raced down the hall.

"Hello, boy." Wiggins's muffled voice could be heard. A moment later, he popped into the room. "It's done. The inspector and Constable Barnes is on their way."

"I take it the inspector believed your story?" Mrs. Jeffries asked. To her way of thinking, that was the key.

"He believed me all right. But Inspector

Nivens was givin' me some funny looks."

"Nivens was there?" Mrs. Jeffries didn't like the sound of that.

"It's a funny thing." Wiggins frowned. "'E spotted me comin' in the building as 'e was leavin', but instead of goin' on about 'is business, 'e turned heel and followed me right up to the inspector's desk. 'Ung about the whole time I was there."

"That's not good." Smythe shot the housekeeper a worried look.

"It most certainly isn't."

"You think he's onto us?" Luty asked.

"I don't know," Mrs. Jeffries admitted honestly. "But the fact that he followed Wiggins back inside is worrying."

"We'll 'ave to be doubly careful, won't we?" Smythe said. "Sounds to me like Nivens is going to be watchin' this investigation pretty sharp like."

"That's true," Betsy said brightly. "But he'll only be concerned about the murdered man. He doesn't know about Miss Gentry. So the only people who have to be careful are you and Wiggins."

Mrs. Jeffries had a cold supper laid in the dining room and was standing at the ready when Inspector Witherspoon came home. "Good evening, sir."

"Good evening, Mrs. Jeffries. I'm so sorry to be late."

"That's quite all right, sir." She reached for his bowler. "We expected you wouldn't be home on time for dinner. Wiggins told us what happened. I've a cold supper laid out, sir."

"Would it be too much trouble if we had a glass of sherry first?" Witherspoon asked hopefully.

"That would be splendid, sir," she replied. Her spirits soared. She couldn't believe her good luck. An invitation for a sherry together was a sure sign the inspector wanted to have one of his "chats" about the case.

They went into the drawing room and Witherspoon dropped into his favorite armchair. The lamps had already been lighted and the room was suffused with a pale, golden glow. Mrs. Jeffries went to the mahogany sideboard and got the elegant Waterford crystal sherry glasses off of the top shelf. She pulled open the bottom cabinet and removed a bottle of Harvey's. She filled both glasses to the brim. Putting her sherry on the table next to the settee, she handed the inspector his glass. "Here you are, sir. Just what the doctor ordered after a long, hard day at work." She wanted to get right onto the subject at hand. "It must have been a really dreadful day for you, sir."

"Perhaps, but it was a great deal worse for the poor fellow who got himself strangled." He took a quick gulp of his drink.

She pretended to be surprised. "Strangled? Oh dear, you mean he was murdered? All Wiggins said was he'd seen a dead body. He seemed so upset, we didn't press him for details; we just assumed that whoever it was had died of natural causes."

"I'm afraid not. There was quite a wide ligature mark about the fellow's throat." He shuddered.

"How very sad, sir." She clucked her tongue sympathetically. "I don't suppose you've been able to identify him?"

"Oh yes, that was quite easy. His name was Stanley McIntosh. He was a caretaker of a grammar school. Which, by the way, has been closed since Easter."

"So he was strangled, sir?"

"It certainly looked like it."

"Do you have any idea who might have murdered the poor man?" She asked this as a matter of course.

He sighed. "Not as yet. We sent police constables to do a house-to-house in the local area, but so far, we've not turned up much."

"Did this Mr. McIntosh live in the school itself?"

"He had a room off the kitchen. Actually, they'd converted the dry larder into a bedroom for the fellow. We searched the room but we came up with nothing."

"Could robbery have been the motive, sir?" she asked innocently.

"I doubt it, the school is virtually nothing more than an empty shell and the victim had nothing of value in his room. Quite sad, really, nothing but a few old rags for clothes and some postcards he'd kept under his bed in a cigar box." He closed his eyes and shook his head. "Not much to show for a man's life. But whatever modest means he had, however humble his position and circumstances, no one had the right to kill him. To take his life."

"I agree, sir," she said softly. From any other man, the sentiment expressed by him would have sounded false or silly, but Mrs. Jeffries knew he meant every single word. He would do everything in his power to bring the killer to justice. "I know you'll catch the murderer, sir. You always do."

"I certainly hope so, Mrs. Jeffries. But I

must admit, I'm not overly optimistic about our chances. There seems no reason for this killing."

"But there never seems to be a reason for murder, sir," she protested. "Not in the beginning of a case. What's got you so pessimistic about this one?"

He smiled wanly. "I don't really know. There was just something so depressing about the whole situation. Here was this poor wretch of a man living in that awful little room. There weren't any curtains, or pictures or books or carpeting or anything to brighten his miserable existence, just this silly cigar box with a few postcards that he'd probably drug out of dustbins." He sighed and shook his head again. "Why would anyone want to kill someone who had so little? It seems so pointless and cruel, I simply don't understand, Mrs. Jeffries."

Mrs. Jeffries gazed at him sympathetically. He really was a sensitive person. She understood exactly what he meant. "Life is often cruel, Inspector," she said softly. "And it's because of this random misery that what you do is so important. You'll find the person who took this McIntosh's life and you'll put them in prison so they can't ever hurt anyone again."

"I'm flattered by your faith in me." He sighed again, but this time he didn't sound quite so depressed. "I only hope I can justify it."

"You've never failed in the past, sir," she reminded him, "and there's no reason to think you'll fail on this case. Now, sir, do tell me what you've learned so far. You know how I love hearing all the details." She held her breath, hoping she'd managed to shift his mood.

He hesitated for a moment and then he swallowed the bait. "Well, we did learn a few things today. There weren't any witnesses, of course, but one of the neighbors said they'd seen Mr. McIntosh crossing the school yard earlier today."

"Earlier today?" she repeated. She wanted something a bit more specific.

"Around a quarter to eleven." Witherspoon took another drink of sherry. "So far, that's the last time anyone saw him alive."

"Except for the killer," she said. "It would have been nice if your witness had seen someone going into the school yard."

"That would certainly make my task a great deal easier." He drained his glass and got to his feet. "Perhaps we'll come up with something soon. Not all of the lads doing the house-to-house had reported in by the time I left the station. So there's still hope. Someone may have seen something."

Mrs. Jeffries suddenly remembered that Smythe and Wiggins had been at the school. She hoped it wouldn't be their bad luck that someone had seen one of them. But she managed to give the inspector an encouraging smile. "Let's hope so, sir. Did you find any evidence of what actually, uh, strangled the victim?" She might as well get as many details as possible.

Witherspoon started toward the dining room. "We think the killer must have used rope. The marks on the throat certainly weren't caused by hands."

"Why do you think it was rope, sir?" she asked as she followed him into the dining room.

Witherspoon pulled out his chair and sat down. "There was a length of it tossed into the corner. Of course, we won't know the cause of death until the postmortem is completed. But Dr. Bosworth assured me that he'll have the results by tomorrow."

Mrs. Jeffries's spirits lifted. "Dr. Bosworth. He's doing the autopsy?"

"Oh yes; Dr. Potter's gout has flared up again and the district doctor's got a broken

96

arm. I had Barnes send over to St. Thomas's for Dr. Bosworth. I'm sure the chief inspector won't object. It's not good to delay the postmortem, you know. I mean" — he yanked his serviette off the table and onto his lap — "we think the man was strangled, but we don't know for certain, if you get my meaning."

"Yes, sir, I believe I do," Mrs. Jeffries agreed. She deliberately kept her expression casual, but she was delighted that Dr. Bosworth would be doing the autopsy. He'd helped them on several of the inspector's cases.

"I'm not very hungry," the inspector said as he reached for his fork, "but I suppose I should eat something."

"Absolutely, sir," she assured him. "You must keep up your strength. You've much to do in the next few days."

Smythe had the uncomfortable feeling that someone was watching him as he slipped around the corner of Orley Road. Yet when he looked over his shoulder, he saw nothing. "I'm gettin' fanciful," he muttered to himself. Yet the feeling persisted as he continued up the road and around the bend to a pub he'd spotted. It was a plain, honest workingman's pub called the

White Hare. He pushed into the public bar and took a good, long look around before moving up to the bar. "I'll have a pint of your best bitter," he told the publican.

The room was crowded with workers, shop assistants, day laborers, and even a few bank clerks in their suits and ties.

"Here you are." The barman slid his glass of beer across the counter.

"Ta." Smythe slapped down his money, picked up his beer, and headed toward an empty chair in the corner. "This spot taken?" he asked a ruddy-faced man sitting at the table.

"It's yours if you want it," the fellow replied.

Smythe sat down and sipped his beer. He didn't try to start a conversation, he simply sat there keeping his ears open.

"Blast and damn, that bitch's got a sharp tongue," the man at the table next to him said to his companion. "A bit late with the ready and she's wantin' to toss me out on me ear."

"You know how women are," his companion replied, "they want to know the rent's been paid. Can't blame her for that."

Thinking this conversation wasn't particularly interesting, Smythe turned his head slightly, the better to hear the conversation going on behind him.

"Ada told me she weren't in the least surprised old McIntosh got done in, what with him bein' such a secretive sort." The voice was female and sharp.

Smythe turned his head and looked behind him. Two women were sitting at the table in the corner. One had frizzy blond hair stuck up in a knot on the top of her head and the other had dark brown hair. It was the frizzy blonde that was doing the talking. "He might have looked as poor as a church mouse, but believe me, he could come up with the money when he —" She broke off as she saw Smythe staring at her.

He decided to plunge straight ahead. There was no point in being coy. "Sorry," he said quickly, "I couldn't 'elp over-hearin'. Are you talkin' about that poor bloke that got 'imself murdered yesterday?"

Frizzy blonde cocked her head to one side and appraised him shrewdly. "What's it to you?"

Smythe suddenly realized the entire room had gone quiet. He wasn't sure what to do next. He looked around the room and noticed that people weren't just staring at him curiously, there was open hostility on most of their faces. "I was just wonderin'," he finally said. "Bein' curious, that's all."

"You'd do best to mind your own business," the man at his own table said. "Being too curious about Stan McIntosh can get a man killed."

Smythe wasn't going to let this lot intimidate him. He stared hard at the man who'd spoken until the fellow looked away. The others turned back to their own business.

Blast, he thought, there goes my chance to get anything out of this lot. Asking any more questions here would be a waste of his time. These people had closed ranks. Something was going on. Something the police wouldn't have a hope in Hades of getting out of any of them. If he wanted to find out what was happening here, there was only one thing left for him to do.

He'd have to make a trip to the East End docks.

He needed to see Blimpey Groggins.

Chapter 4

"They're the most awful gossips," Ida Leahcock said to Mrs. Goodge. "They'd talk the hind legs off a dog, they would. Those tea cakes are very nice, Mrs. Goodge, begging your pardon. I don't suppose you'd part with the recipe, would you?"

The cook hesitated, torn between hoarding her own precious recipes and wanting to keep Ida talking. "Of course you can have it," she said with a bright smile. "Please, do help yourself to another." She'd give Ida the recipe all right, minus an important ingredient or two. "Now, you were saying about the Adderly twins, the ones that was going on and on about that Reverend Cook."

"Reverend Cooksey," Ida corrected as she reached across the table and snatched up another tea cake. She was a thin, sparse woman with steel-gray hair done up in a skinny bun, a pointy nose, and a pair of sharp brown eyes that could spot a pickpocket or a petty thief at twenty paces. On the back of her right hand she had a birthmark in the shape of a hedgehog. "Eliza Adderly was the one that told me all about him. Mind you, she only found out because she works for the Cookseys and she happened to overhear Mrs. Cooksey giving the reverend a right earful." She paused long enough to stuff half the tea cake into her mouth.

Mrs. Goodge forced herself to keep smiling. She wasn't going to let the woman's piggish manners put her off. It wasn't often in an investigation that information as good as this dropped right into her lap, so to speak. Well, it hadn't exactly dropped into her lap; she'd sent a street Arab with a note over to invite Ida to tea after learning the Cookseys lived in Hammersmith.

Ida Leahcock owned Lanhams, a café just outside the Shepherd's Bush station. Every working person in the area stopped in for tea. Ida knew them all. Back more years than she liked to remember, Mrs. Goodge and Ida had once been kitchen maids together. Mrs. Goodge had minded her work, kept herself decent, and climbed the ranks to end up a highly respected cook. Ida had been caught kissing a stable boy in the back garden and tossed out without a reference. But that hadn't stopped her from being successful. She'd ended up owning half a dozen small, but lucrative cafés. Mrs. Goodge had run into the woman at the greengrocer's one morning. They'd both been reaching for the same apple. She recognized the hedgehog birthmark on Ida's hand right away. It hadn't taken more than five minutes of chat before Mrs. Goodge realized that Ida Leahcock, the kitchen maid dismissed in scandal all those years ago, was now a successful businesswoman. More importantly, she was a walking gold mine of information. "An earful?" Mrs. Goodge prompted.

Ida snickered. "Apparently she doesn't have much respect for his being a man of the cloth. I heard the two of them had a right old slinging match, they did. Eliza told me she almost run out of the house in fright as they was screaming at each other so loud. Mind you, Eliza's a bit of twit. Scared of her own shadow, she is. You know what I mean. Remember that green girl that worked at Morgan's with us? The one with the buckteeth and the runny nose. Eliza reminds me of her."

Mrs. Goodge didn't have a clue whom Ida was referring to but she'd die a thousand deaths rather than admit her memory wasn't as keen as the other woman's. "Indeed I do," she said heartily. "Frightened of the wind, she was."

Ida nodded in agreement. "That's right. Well, Eliza didn't run outside, she just hid in the kitchen until the shouting died down. She may be a ninny, but she wanted her wages and this happened on the last day of the quarter."

"What were they arguing about, anyway?" Mrs. Goodge reached for the teapot and poured more tea for Ida.

"Ta. Seems that Mrs. Cooksey was giving the reverend what for about him being out of a position. Said she couldn't hold her head up no more and that he ought to be ashamed of himself for not being able to provide for his wife."

"I've never heard of such a thing!" Mrs. Goodge clucked her tongue in disapproval. "You don't say — a vicar out of work. Doesn't the church have to find them a parish?"

"That's what I always thought," Ida said. "But maybe it's not true."

Mrs. Goodge made a mental note to find out exactly how the Church of England's bishops appointed vicars. There was something amiss here, she could feel it. "Maybe there's just too many vicars and not enough parishes," she suggested.

"That's not it." Ida waved her hand dismissively. "He's probably had his hand in the till or been messing about with the choirboys. Mark my words, it'll be scandal that's got him out of a job."

Mrs. Goodge tried to look shocked, but the truth was, she really wasn't. She'd once believed that people in positions of authority were true and good and honorable. But since she'd gotten involved in investigating murders, she'd found it was often those people in authority who lied, cheated, and worst of all, killed.

"That's usually how these things turn out," Ida continued cheerfully.

"Didn't Eliza have any idea why he'd not got a parish?"

"That silly goose," Ida snorted. "Even after hearing that screaming match, Eliza still thinks the good reverend is taking a long rest for his health."

Smythe scowled at the two pickpockets standing in front of the Admiral Nelson pub. Blast, he thought as the two scurried out of his way, trust Blimpey to pick a place not fit for man nor beast.

The pub was in the East End, on St. George Street. It was close enough to the Tobacco Dock to smell it. This was an area of London that reeked of poverty and was plagued with crime, misery, and pain. The only good thing that ever came out of here, he thought as he elbowed his way through the crowded public bar, was Betsy. He knew she'd been born not far from here. He thanked God every day that she'd gotten out and landed on the inspector's doorstep. He refused even to think of what her life would have been like if she'd stayed in the East End.

He heard a familiar laugh. Turning, he spotted a portly man with ginger-colored hair sitting at one of the few tables. Blimpey saw him and winked.

"Nice to see you, my friend." Blimpey patted the chair next to him. The day was warm but he had a bright red scarf dangling around his neck over his dirty brown-and-white-checkered coat. A battered porkpie hat was sitting forlornly on the table. "It's been a while since you and I've crossed paths."

Smythe raised an eyebrow. "It's not been that long. What'll you have?" he asked, glancing at Blimpey's empty glass. He knew the rules. Blimpey expected to be well supplied while you conducted business.

"Gin." Blimpey nodded at the barman. "And bring us two pints of the best bitter as well. You still drink beer, don't you?"

"That'll be fine." Smythe yanked out the chair and sat down. "I've just not got a lot of time."

"You're always in a hurry," Blimpey chided him. "That's what's wrong with this world, people are always in a bloody rush. They ought to slow down a bit, take time to exchange a few kind words with their fellowman."

Smythe rolled his eyes. "The only thing you ever exchange with your fellowman is a bit of coin. Now let's get down to it. I've got someone I want you to find out about. Fellow is named Stan McIntosh —"

"The bloke that got killed?" Blimpey's cheerful grin vanished.

"How'd you hear about it? It's not been in the papers."

Blimpey gave him a pitying look and Smythe realized how stupid he sounded. Of course Blimpey had heard about the murder. Blimpey heard about everything criminal in this town. That's why Smythe had come to him. The man had been a petty thief, but he'd soon realized that his incredible memory could earn him a great deal more than simple thieving. Besides, thievery was a dangerous occupation. Blimpey had a natural distaste for violence and an ability to organize snippets of information that went far beyond his meager education. Before you could say "Bob's-your-uncle," he had a network of informants that stretched from Spitalfields to Putney. He collected information the way a dog collected fleas. Then he sold it to whoever would pay for it. Smythe was one of his best customers.

"Why are you so interested in this McIntosh?" Blimpey eyed him speculatively.

"Here ya are, fellers." A buxom barmaid put their drinks on the table. "A gin and two pints of the best."

"Thanks." Smythe reached into his shirt pocket, took out some coins, and handed them to the woman.

"Thanks," she replied when she saw what he'd given her. She rushed off before he could ask for change.

He stared steadily at Blimpey. He wasn't about to answer questions as to why he wanted information. That wasn't part of their arrangement. But despite his scowl, he didn't blame the fellow for trying it on. Gathering information was the man's stock-in-trade.

Blimpey gave in gracefully. "No harm in askin'. A healthy curiosity is what makes life worth livin'. That's what I always say. You need the goods on anyone else?"

Smythe hesitated. He knew he shouldn't be sticking his oar in the Gentry investigation. After all, it had been his suggestion that they separate the murder from the attempted murder. But as he was here anyway, why not get his money's worth. "Yeah, there is." He thought for a moment, trying to recall all the names that had been bandied about the kitchen during their meeting. "Find out what you can about some people who live over in Hammersmith and Kensington."

"What's the names?"

"Reverend Harold Cooksey and his wife, Louisa. They live in Hammersmith. The other one's a barrister and his wife by the name of Caraway —"

"Elliot Caraway?" Blimpey interrupted.

"You've heard of 'im?" Smythe was shocked.

Blimpey sneered. "He took the brief for a friend of mine in a stolen-goods case. Poor bloke was innocent but he ended up doing six years in the Scrubs."

"Bad luck," Smythe murmured.

"Luck had nothin' to do with it." Blimpey's eyes flashed angrily. "Caraway's an idiot and poor Rysington got six years for a crime he didn't commit. And it weren't the first time it had happened, either. Word I got is Caraway's so bad he can't get criminal briefs at all anymore. Stupid old git."

"Well, find out what you can about the bloke and about the other names I give you." He threw back the rest of his beer and started to get up, when he remembered there'd been another guest in Miss Gentry's house the day the dog had been poisoned. "And find out what you can about a fellow named Eddington, too. Phillip Eddington."

"Where does 'e live?" Blimpey asked.

"I'm not sure . . . wait a minute, it's on Forest Street. On the other side of St. Matthew's Church."

"Right." Blimpey finished off his gin and got to his feet. "Meet me back here tomorrow evening around eight, I ought to have something for ya by then."

"I knew that this case was going to be quite difficult, Constable," Witherspoon said to Barnes as they made their way down Forest Street. "I had a bad feeling about it."

"You always think that, sir," Barnes replied, "and we always end up solvin' the case. Besides, sir, we've done quite well. At least we found one person who had business dealings with the deceased. It's a start, isn't it?"

"Yes." Witherspoon sighed and started up the steps of a large, Georgian house. "We've got a place to begin. Let's see what this Mr. Eddington may know." He banged the heavy brass knocker against the polished white door.

The door opened a moment later. "Yes? Can I help you?" A gray-haired woman wearing a soiled white apron and holding a cleaning rag in her hand stared curiously at Barnes.

"We'd like to see Mr. Eddington," Witherspoon said. "We're —"

"Who is it, Jane?" a voice from inside the house interrupted.

"It's the coppers," Jane screeched. She threw the door open wide.

Witherspoon winced then quickly recovered as a middle-aged man with dark curly hair worn straight back from his broad face came down the wide hall. "Why, goodness, it *is* the police." He sounded very surprised.

"They want to see you, sir," Jane said, eager to learn more.

"Thank you, Jane, you may go now and

finish cleaning the stove. I'll see the gentlemen into the drawing room."

Jane's round, eager face crumbled in disappointment. Then she nodded glumly and shuffled off toward the back of the house. Eddington turned back to the policemen. "Gentlemen, do come in."

"Thank you." Witherspoon and Barnes stepped inside the foyer. "I do hate to trouble you, sir, but we'd like to ask you a few questions regarding a Mr. Stanley McIntosh."

"Who?"

"I take it you are Phillip Eddington?" Witherspoon wanted to make sure he was talking to the right person.

"I am, indeed." He frowned slightly. "But I don't know what this is all about. Perhaps we ought to gointo the drawing room." He turned and led the way.

They followed; their footsteps sounded loud on the polished wood floor. They went through a double oak door into a formal drawing room. It was large and pleasant but not opulently furnished. There was a plain brown settee with a matching set of chairs. Several tables, a bookcase full of books on the end wall, plain white muslin curtains at the windows, and framed hunting prints on the walls. "Do please sit down," Eddington instructed, gesturing at the settee.

As soon as they'd sat down, Constable Barnes whipped out his little brown notebook. He looked expectantly at his superior.

Witherspoon cleared his throat. "I'm Inspector Gerald Witherspoon and this is Constable Barnes. We've come to ask you a few questions regarding Mr. Stanley McIntosh. He was the caretaker at Helmsley's Grammar School. We've reason to believe that you knew Mr. McIntosh."

Clearly puzzled, Eddington stared at them for a few moments and then his expression brightened in understanding. "Oh, you're talking about old Stan. Of course, how silly of me. I'm sorry. I didn't quite realize who you meant. I did know him, actually. As a matter of fact, I saw him just yesterday. What's this all about, inspector? Is he in some sort of trouble?"

His voice had a slight inflection to it, one that the inspector couldn't quite place. Almost, but not quite, an accent. "What was your business with Mr. McIntosh, sir?"

"I would hardly call it business, Inspector. More like charity." Eddington shrugged. "I felt sorry for the poor chap. He'd mentioned the board of governors at

Helmsley's had found a buyer for the property and his job might be coming to an end. I wanted to see if he wanted some work."

"He was going to lose his position?" Witherspoon wondered why the secretary of the board of governors hadn't mentioned that fact when they'd spoken earlier today.

"That's what he told me." Eddington smiled kindly. "I'm sorry, I didn't really know him very well. But, you know how it is, I'd seen him in passing and I'd spoken to him a time or two, exchanged pleasantries, that sort of thing. The last time we spoke, he mentioned that he was going to be out of work. I've got a bit of painting that needs to be done around here and I thought he might like a go at it. It's not exactly a position, but I thought it might help him make ends meet until he could find another job."

"So you went over to the school to see if he wanted to work for you?" the inspector clarified.

"That's right." Eddington relaxed back against the cushions.

"What time was this, sir?" Constable Barnes asked.

"Oh" — Eddington's face creased

thoughtfully — "let me see, it must have been about eleven-thirty or so. Oh dear, I'm not exactly sure what time it was. But it was late in the morning. Before noon."

"You saw Mr. McIntosh?"

He shook his head. "Actually, no. I stuck my head in the back door and called out, but there was no answer. I tried several times but I never found the fellow. What's all this about, Inspector?"

"I'm afraid the reason Mr. McIntosh never answered you was because he was dead."

Eddington's mouth gaped open. "Dead? Gracious, that's terrible."

"Sorry to say, he was murdered, sir. That's why we're here making inquiries."

They met back at Upper Edmonton Gardens at four o'clock for their meeting. Betsy was the last to arrive. "I'm sorry to be so late," she said, tossing her beloved one of her warm smiles as she rushed across the kitchen to put away her things. "But I was doing ever so well."

"That's excellent, Betsy," Mrs. Jeffries said. She was sitting at the head of the table. "Hurry and sit down so we can get started. It looks as if we've all something to report."

"I don't," Smythe admitted easily. "So far I've not turned up a ruddy thing." He didn't mind letting the others have their moment of glory. His turn would be coming. Blimpey hadn't failed him yet and he had no doubt he'd give them an earful at tomorrow's meeting.

"Well, who's gonna go first?" Luty asked eagerly. Since she was bouncing up and down in her chair, it was obvious to everyone she was bursting to talk.

"Patience, madam," Hatchet said. "We'll all have our say in good time."

"I think we ought to let Luty talk," Wiggins said. "Looks to me like she's got somethin' real interestin' to tell us."

"That's right nice of you, boy." Luty patted his arm. "And I do have somethin' interestin' to say. But I expect the rest of you do, too."

Mrs. Jeffries poured Betsy's tea and handed it to her as the maid took her place next to Smythe. She'd seen the warm, intimate smile the girl had given the coachman and was delighted the two of them were getting along so well. Sometimes on their investigations, Betsy had a tendency to be too competitive with him and Smythe could be a tad overprotective of her. "If everyone else agrees, why don't you go first, Luty."

"Seein' as how no one is raisin' a fuss, I believe I will." She paused to take a deep breath. "As this case is gettin' complicated, I made me out a list." She pulled a rolled-up piece of paper out of the bright red sleeve of her dress. "I know we decided to keep things separate, but I had old Teddyworth's ear, so I decided to kill two birds with one stone and find out all I could about the people in both situations."

"Huh?" Wiggins said. "Who's Teddyworth?"

"One of Madam's bankers," Hatchet said smoothly. "He's well connected in the City."

"Thank you, Hatchet," Luty said tartly. Turning her head, she gave the butler a wide smile. "I did a little checking into our murder victim's finances."

Hatchet snorted. "He was a caretaker, madam. He could hardly have had 'finances' as far as the City was concerned."

"Fat lot you know," Luty shot back. "He had a deposit account at the West London Commercial Bank over on Sloane Square. Had a hundred and thirty-five pounds in it."

"I stand corrected, madam," Hatchet said loftily. "Now we know that the man had a veritable fortune, I'm sure we should conclude that's the reason he was murdered. Do tell us who his beneficiaries might be."

"Hatchet, you don't have to be so sarcastic," Luty said. "I know it ain't a fortune. But it's something. Now, if it's all the same to you, I'll get on with my report. This McIntosh fellow wasn't the only one I found out about." She squinted at the paper she'd just unrolled. "Our Miss Gentry has plenty, too. Her fortune's valued at a hundred thousand pounds."

"Gracious, that *is* an enormous amount." Mrs. Jeffries wasn't sure what this meant, but she knew it meant something. That much money often attracted trouble.

"Just so you'll know, I did a bit of snoopin' about Miss Gentry, wanted to make sure we could trust her, if you know what I mean," Luty continued. "She was livin' on the edge of poverty, gettin' by all these years on a tiny inheritance from her mother, when all of a sudden the woman who would have been her mother-in-law up and dies and leaves her sittin' pretty."

"Exactly how did Mrs. Dempsey die?" Mrs. Goodge asked.

It was Mrs. Jeffries who answered. "Pneumonia. I already checked. The death wasn't considered suspicious. She was over eighty and had been ill a long time."

"Annabeth Gentry took care of Mrs. Dempsey," Betsy protested. "She had no idea of what Mrs. Dempsey was worth; no one did."

"I ain't sayin' she killed the old woman," Luty said. "I'm just sayin' how she come to have all that cash. It's no wonder someone's tryin' to kill her."

"Money isn't the only motive for murder," Smythe put in. "Just because Miss Gentry inherited a bundle doesn't mean that's the reason someone's tryin' to do 'er in."

"It's a darned good motive, though," Luty argued.

"I still think it's got somethin' to do with her findin' that Tim Porter," Wiggins put in. "That's when it began."

"I agree," Mrs. Jeffries said.

"But yesterday you said we ought to keep things separate," Mrs. Goodge reminded her.

"I know. But after thinking about it all night, I changed my opinion. But let's let Luty finish and then we can discuss it."

"Thank you, Hepzibah," Luty said. "Now, as I was sayin', Annabeth Gentry inherited an estate big enough to choke a horse —"

"When, exactly, did she get this inheritance?" The housekeeper wanted to get the facts straight in her mind.

"About six months ago," Luty replied.

"Who stands to inherit from Miss Gentry?" Smythe asked softly.

"I don't know," Luty admitted. "But as she ain't married, it's probably her sisters."

"We need to find out for certain," Mrs. Jeffries said. "It could well be important."

"I've got my sources workin' on that very question," Mrs. Goodge said.

"Excellent," Mrs. Jeffries said. "Then we can continue. Luty, anything else?"

"Only that the Caraways are broke," Luty replied. "I've still got my sources" — she shot the cook a quick grin — "workin' on finding out if the good reverend's broke, too, but I haven't heard back from them yet."

"If you're finished, madam," Hatchet interjected, "I'd like to speak next."

"I'm done," she replied.

Hatchet smiled apologetically at the others. "Do forgive me for jumping in, but I believe my information might complement madam's quite nicely."

"Go on," Mrs. Jeffries said.

"As you'll recall, my task was to go to Miss Gentry's soon-to-be new abode on Forest Street and ask about. I must say, I wasn't overly enthusiastic about the assignment, but on the whole, I must admit it went rather well . . . it's quite amazing what the local people know."

"Local people? For goodness' sakes, it's only a quarter of a mile from where she lives now," Luty said impatiently.

"I know that, madam," he chided. "I'm simply trying to give everyone a bit of understanding about the circumstances. We've all admitted this is going to be a most complicated case."

"Yes, Hatchet, that's true," Mrs. Jeffries said. "It's very complex." But she rather agreed with Luty, Hatchet was being very long-winded.

"Thank you." He smiled at the housekeeper. Luty snorted softly. "As I was saying, it's quite amazing what the local people can tell you. I had a most enlightening conversation with one Mr. Jonathan Parradom, one of the local tradesmen."

"What did you find out?" Mrs. Jeffries's voice was just the slightest bit impatient.

"It seems that Miss Gentry's troubles didn't start with the attempts on her life; she's also had a terrible run of bad luck on getting her new home refurbished."

"What do you mean?" Mrs. Goodge asked. "Everyone has troubles with builders."

"Miss Gentry was due to move into the place at the beginning of this month. But in the past two weeks, she's been delayed. First by a flood in the kitchen and then by a fire on the upper floors."

"Both of these things have happened since her dog found Tim Porter's body?" Mrs. Jeffries mused.

Hatchet nodded slowly. "Once I heard that, I, too, began to think that it all must be connected somehow. No one has this much bad luck."

"We need to be careful here," Mrs. Jeffries warned. "Remember, we've made assumptions in other cases and the results weren't what we'd hoped." In one awful case, by acting on theories that appeared to be true but really weren't, they'd done very badly in their investigation. Why, they'd actually had the case solved by the inspector with virtually no help from them. Mrs. Jeffries was determined that this wasn't going to happen again. "But, still, my instincts are telling me it's all connected somehow."

Betsy sighed. "We've got to keep our minds sharp."

"Agreed," Hatchet said somberly.

"Have you finished?" Mrs. Jeffries asked.

"Yes, I believe so." Hatchet sighed. He'd picked up another rumor or two, but after hearing Mrs. Jeffries's warning, he decided to determine if they were true before he confided in the others. They really must be on their guard.

"I've got some bits to tell," Mrs. Goodge said before anyone else could speak up. "I found out that it's true that Reverend Cooksey doesn't have a parish. Furthermore, it's not by choice." She gave them all the details she'd learned from Ida Leahcock. When she finished, she poured herself another cup of tea.

"So if 'e doesn't 'ave a church," Wiggins asked, " 'ow's he makin' a livin'?"

"He could be independently wealthy," Hatchet suggested.

"If he was wealthy, why would his wife be shouting at him about being a bad provider," Betsy pointed out. "Besides, I found a few things about the Cookseys today, too, and about the Caraways. They've been trying to get Miss Gentry to turn control of her inheritance over to one of her brother-in-laws ever since Mrs. Dempsey died. But she's having none of it. She's handling it herself."

"Good for her. Did you find out anything else?" Mrs. Jeffries asked.

"A bit," Betsy replied. "Miss Gentry is well liked about the neighborhood. All the tradesmen and shopkeepers have nothing but good to say about her."

"Excellent, Betsy. Is that it?" The maid nodded her head, and Mrs. Jeffries turned her attention to Wiggins. "How about you? Did you find out any more about Stan McIntosh?"

"A little," Wiggins replied. "McIntosh pretty much kept to 'imself. The local people didn't know too much about 'im. 'E took care of the school grounds and tried to keep the place from fallin' apart until the board of governors can sell the property."

"Has he been there a long time?" Mrs. Goodge took another sip of tea.

"No one knew exactly 'ow long," Wiggins said. "But I know 'e was workin' there while it still 'ad pupils. The locals didn't know much about the feller. I think I ought to find out if any of the staff or students from the school is still about the area."

"What good would that do?" Mrs. Goodge asked.

Wiggins shrugged. "Maybe one of the

students would know something about McIntosh. Children are right nosy, you know. They know all sorts of things."

"I think that's a splendid idea," Mrs. Jeffries said. "Until we learn something more about the victim, we'll never find out how these cases are connected."

"Can I go next?" Smythe asked.

"I thought you said you didn't have anything to report," Betsy said. She watched his face suspiciously. It would be just like the man to pretend like he'd not got a thing and then to drop a big surprise on them.

"I don't," he said earnestly. "I mean, I don't have any facts. But somethin' odd 'appened and I think you ought to know about it."

"What is it?"

Smythe told them about his visit to the local pub. About how the locals had not only closed ranks, but had been openly hostile. "I don't know what got their backs up," he finished. "I was bein' right careful in what I said. Do you think it's important?"

Mrs. Jeffries thought about it for a moment before she answered. "I'm not sure. It could just be the natural inclination of a group to close ranks against an outsider —"

"It's important," Hatchet said. "Oh, I'm sorry, Mrs. Jeffries, I didn't mean to interrupt you."

"That's quite all right." She waved his apology away. "But I am curious as to your reasons."

"Yeah, so am I," Luty added.

"Well," Hatchet began, "Smythe was in a pub. Now, it was probably the local, but pubs are used to having people come and go. And in a case like this, a case of murder, everyone in the place should have been talking about it. But they weren't. I find that very strange."

"So do I," Smythe said. "And I think I'll make it my business to find out why everyone got so niggled just by my mentionin' McIntosh's name."

"Be careful, Smythe," Betsy said. "I've got a bad feeling about it." The words slipped out before she could stop herself. She was always trying to stop him from being overprotective of her and here she was doing the same to him.

He gave her a knowing grin. She could feel a flush creeping up her cheeks.

"I'm sure Smythe will take great care," Mrs. Jeffries soothed.

"Now, does anyone else have anything to add?" She waited a moment but no one spoke. "As I said earlier, I think we now ought to proceed with our investigation based on the assumption that all these events are somehow connected."

"But you warned us not to jump to conclusions," Mrs. Goodge protested. "You pointed out that we'd been wrong in the past when we did that."

"I know." Mrs. Jeffries wasn't sure how to explain this part. "But I've given this a great deal of thought and it's the timing that makes me believe everything is connected. Nothing happened until Miranda found that body. Then, all of a sudden, Miss Gentry has three attempts made on her life, her new house has a fire and a flood, and there's another murder less than a hundred yards from where she lives. I don't think it's a coincidence. But I'm willing to change my opinion if the rest of you think I'm wrong."

"I think you're right," Luty said softly. "Like was said earlier, no one has as much bad luck as Miss Gentry unlessin' there's someone behind it."

"I agree," Betsy said. "There's someone behind all this."

"And it ain't goin' to be easy to find out who it is," Smythe added.

"We'll find 'em," Wiggins said cheerfully. "We always do."

"Right, then." Mrs. Jeffries smiled at the others. "We go forward on the assumption that the cases are connected. Does anyone else have anything they'd like to report?"

No one did. But they stayed on for another half hour going over the details of the cases and deciding on what they'd do next. By the time Luty and Hatchet left, it was getting dark. Mrs. Jeffries didn't expect the inspector home for dinner until quite late. She felt quite safe going upstairs to her rooms to have a think about everything they'd discussed.

But she was only halfway up the landing when she heard the front door open. "Hello, hello," Witherspoon called out cheerfully.

Mrs. Jeffries turned and hurried back down the stairs. "Hello, sir. I didn't expect you home till much later."

"I thought I'd pop in to have a bit of supper," he explained as he took off his bowler. "I've a brief meeting this evening with Chief Inspector Barrows. He wants a report on the case."

"Isn't that an odd time to be seeing your chief inspector?" she asked. She spotted Betsy coming up the stairs. As soon as the maid realized the inspector had come home early, she did an about-face and went back the way she'd just come. Mrs. Jeffries was confident that the girl would tell the cook to prepare a tray.

"Usually, yes, but he's going to Birmingham tomorrow and wanted to get a report before he left. Er, do you think Mrs. Goodge will be able to put something together for me? I'm quite hungry."

"I'm sure we can get you a decent meal, sir," she replied. "If you'd like to go into the drawing room, I'll bring some tea while you're waiting." She hurried down to the kitchen. Betsy and Mrs. Goodge were busy preparing a cold supper.

"I've some cold chicken and half a loaf of bread," the cook said. "It'll have to do."

"Don't you have any of those treacle tarts left?" Betsy asked. "I saw some in the larder earlier today."

Mrs. Goodge hesitated. "Well, all right, I'll give him a tart. But only one. I'm saving the rest for my sources."

Mrs. Jeffries gaped at the cook. For her to hoard her precious tarts for her investigative sources rather than the master of the house was truly a measure of how much she'd changed.

"I know, I know, I really oughtn't to do such a thing," Mrs. Goodge said. "But those treacle tarts get people talking."

"It's all right, Mrs. Goodge," the housekeeper said. "I'll take the tea up. Betsy, bring the tray up in ten minutes."

She took the inspector his tea. "Here you are, sir. Now, how was your day? Did you get any information from the uniformed lads?"

"They did their best, but they didn't learn all that much. But we did have a witness that had seen one of the neighbors in the school yard close to the time the poor fellow must have been killed."

"Really, sir," she said. She silently prayed that the witness hadn't seen Wiggins. Or if it they had, that they'd not given an account that differed too much from what the footman had told the inspector. That could get very awkward.

"Yes, fellow named Phillip Eddington. He lives just on the other side of the church." Witherspoon took a quick sip of his tea.

Mrs. Jeffries tried to remember exactly where she'd heard that name before.

"Nice man, very cooperative. He admitted to going along to see Stan McIntosh that very morning."

"What was his business with the victim?"

"He was trying to help the fellow out." Witherspoon sighed. "He said that

McIntosh had told him that the school was being sold and that he was losing his position. Mr. Eddington had a bit of work for him. Nothing permanent, mind you. Just a bit of painting on the third floor of his home."

"Do you think Mr. Eddington is telling the truth?" Mrs. Jeffries still couldn't remember where she'd heard that name.

The inspector shrugged. "I've no idea. But he doesn't appear to have any reason to dislike McIntosh. I can't imagine why he'd want the fellow dead. Do you think supper will be much longer?"

"I believe I hear Betsy now, sir." She got up and started for the dining room. She was determined to get as much information as possible out of the inspector before he left for the station. "How unfortunate that Mr. Eddington wasn't really all that much help," she said.

"Oh, I wouldn't say that." Witherspoon smiled at Betsy as she put the loaded tray on the dining table. "He gave me the name of someone who'd had some nasty words with McIntosh."

Betsy and Mrs. Jeffries exchanged glances.

"If I didn't have to see the chief inspector this evening, I'd pop along and in-

terview her this very evening," Witherspoon continued as he pulled out a chair
and sat down.

"Her, sir? You mean it's a woman."

"That's right, according to Mr. Eddington, one of the neighbors on the other side
of the school had some rather heated
words with Stan McIntosh only a few days
before he was killed. I believe she accused
him of chucking bricks at her head. Her
name is Gentry. Annabeth Gentry."

Chapter 5

"What'll we do?" Betsy whispered as she and Mrs. Jeffries went down to the kitchen.

"I don't see that we can do anything right at the moment. But I share your concern. We certainly don't want Miss Gentry saying anything to the inspector about us."

Mrs. Goodge looked up as they came into the kitchen. "I thought you were going to keep the inspector company while he ate," she said.

"We've got a bit of a problem," Mrs. Jeffries replied. "We may need Wiggins or Smythe."

"Smythe's gone to the stables," the cook said.

"But I'm 'ere, Mrs. Jeffries." Wiggins, with Fred in tow, walked in from the back hall. From the expressions on their faces, he could tell something was amiss. "What's wrong?"

"The inspector is going to be interviewing Miss Gentry tomorrow about Stan McIntosh," Betsy blurted, "and we don't want her saying anything about us."

"Why on earth would the inspector want to talk to her about him?" Wiggins asked. "We know she didn't 'ave nuthin' to do with him bein' killed. You two was with 'er when the murder took place."

"We can't tell the inspector that we know she didn't do it," Betsy said. "He'd want to know what we were doing there in the first place."

"But this may be just what we want to happen," Mrs. Jeffries exclaimed. "As a matter of fact, I'm sure it is."

"What?" Betsy frowned. "I don't understand. You want the inspector to speak to Miss Gentry?"

"Of course; that's the only way to get this investigation moving along properly. We can only ask questions in the most roundabout of ways. The inspector can actually interrogate people and come up with suspects. In case you've not noticed, we've plenty of murders and attempted murders but virtually no suspects."

"That's the bloomin' truth," the cook muttered. She snapped open a clean tea towel and laid it over the plate of treacle tarts she was hoarding for her sources. "At least if he talks to Miss Gentry, he can start interviewin' those relatives of hers."

"Good, I'm glad you agree. But right

now our immediate concern is to make sure that Miss Gentry says nothing to the inspector about coming to us for help. That's why I'm glad you're here, Wiggins. I want you to nip over to her house and tell her the inspector will be interviewing her tomorrow. Make it clear that she should say nothing about us —" She broke off as she realized she couldn't leave this matter to Wiggins. She'd have to go herself and she'd have to do it tonight. "Never mind. On second thought, I'll have to go over there myself."

"Tonight?" Mrs. Goodge glanced toward the window at the far end of the kitchen. "But it's almost half past six. You haven't had supper yet."

"That's all right, I'll wait till the inspector's gone back to the station and then I'll take a hansom."

"I'll go with ya," Wiggins said. "You don't want to be out at night. They never did catch that Ripper fellow, you know."

"There's no need to do that," she protested. But she was touched nonetheless.

"It's not a good idea for you to be out alone at night," he insisted. "Fred and I'll ride along with ya. We can wait outside if ya like, but I don't think you should go on yer own. Like I said, they never caught that

Ripper bloke. He could still be lurkin' about, and even if 'e's not, there's been two killings in that neighborhood."

"Wiggins is right," Betsy added. "You must take him and Fred."

Mrs. Jeffries gave in gracefully. "All right. Thank you, Wiggins, I'd be pleased to have you and Fred accompany me. I don't think it'll be necessary for you to wait outside, though."

Smythe sidled up to the pub bar and slapped a shilling onto the counter. "What'll you 'ave?" he asked his companion.

"Gin and water," Ned McCluskey replied. He was a young man with dark brown hair, haunted gray eyes, and the look of someone who didn't know where his next meal was coming from. It was a fair assessment of his life. As a simple laborer, he never knew from one day to the next if he'd find work and have money for food.

Smythe nodded at the barman and gave him their orders. When the drinks came, he picked them up and jerked his chin toward an empty table in the corner. "Let's sit down and have a chat."

"Thanks," Ned said as soon as they'd sat

down on the rough wooden stools. He picked up his glass and drained it. "Ahh . . . that's good. It's been so long since I've 'ad a drink."

Smythe sipped his beer. "You can 'ave another, if ya want." He waited for the gray eyes to narrow in suspicion, but Ned was just happy to have a drink. He didn't much care why a complete stranger was buying it for him. "So 'ow long you been workin' at that 'ouse? If you don't mind me askin'?"

Ned shrugged. "Just for the past couple of days. There was a fire up on the third floor and it made an awful bleedin' mess. Boris 'ired me and my mate Jack to clean the rooms and get it ready to be redone and painted."

"A fire? What 'appened?" Smythe deliberately made his own accent more pronounced. He thought Ned would be more open to answering his questions if he thought he was talking to one of his own. He'd had a bit of luck running into the fellow. He'd been on his way back from Howards when he impulsively decided to take a quick look at Annabeth Gentry's new house on Forest Street. He'd spotted Ned and another man coming out the front door. Following them, he'd seen the other man board an omnibus. Ned had started walking. Smythe had caught up with him and struck up a casual conversation. He knew Betsy might worry about him being home so late, but blooming Ada, he couldn't let an opportunity like this pass him by.

"No one actually said what caused the fire." Ned wiped a lock of hair off his forehead. "But Boris seemed to think it were set deliberately."

"Cor blimey," Smythe exclaimed. "Want another gin?"

Ned nodded eagerly and Smythe waved the barmaid over. He was determined to keep the man talking. "Another round 'ere," he told the woman.

"That's right generous of you, mate," Ned said happily. He didn't much care why the big fellow wanted to buy him drinks, he'd keep pouring them down his throat as long as the bloke kept buying. "Now, like I was tellin' ya, Boris thinks the fire were set deliberately."

"Is Boris the boss, then?"

"Oh yeah. He's the guv." He smiled at the barmaid as she put their fresh drinks on the table. "Ta."

Smythe handed her a pound note. "Let me know when this runs out," he said.

"Just give me a nod when you're ready

for another round." She grinned easily.

"Now" — Smythe turned his attention back to Ned — "why does your guv think the fire wasn't an accident?"

"Well, mainly, because of the flood in the kitchen." He grinned. "I know it don't make much sense. But just a week or so before the fire, there was a flood in the ruddy kitchen. The builder told the owner the flood was caused by a loose pipe in the water pump, but that weren't true. Someone had deliberately uncapped the main pipes leadin' from the sink to the wet larder. But the builder wasn't goin' to admit someone 'ad done somethin' daft like that, now, was 'e? For sure the owner woulda blamed it on one of the builder's men and none of 'em would admit to doin' it. So when there was a fire upstairs, Boris nipped up and had a right good look around before Mr. Shoals — that's the builder — could get there. Boris said he couldn't see anythin' up there that could have started a fire like that."

"How would Boris know?" Smythe finished off his beer.

" 'E's got eyes, don't 'e?" Ned replied. " 'E's not stupid. Fires don't just start themselves when there's no reason for that fire to start in the first place."

"What do ya mean?"

"The only people up there that day were the workmen. It was a warm day," he explained. "None of the fireplaces had been used, there weren't any candles or lime lamps or even gas lamps lit. So what could have started it? Boris was curious enough that 'e 'ad a nice long look about the place. 'E found an empty tin of coal oil in the garden, 'e did. He reckoned someone had poured it on the curtains and lit a match."

"Maybe one of the workmen was usin' it for something," Smythe speculated.

"Boris would 'ave known if they'd been usin' coal oil on the job, he's the guv."

"Did Boris tell anyone what he'd found?"

"He told Mr. Shoals and 'e said 'e'd look into it, but I don't think 'e did. He was just happy that the owner didn't make a fuss. Mind you, Shoals isn't a complete fool. 'E's been lucky the owner ain't taken 'im to court over all the damage. 'E finally put a night watchman onto the place right after the fire. Fellow stays there from the time we leave until the morning."

"So there's always someone on the premises?"

"That's right." Ned grinned broadly. "Shoals wasn't worried about the owner so much as 'e was scared somethin' else strange would 'appen. Some barrister fellow did show up after the fire and raised a ruckus. But Miss Gentry, she's the owner, soon quieted the bloke down. Still, it shook Shoals up to 'ave a lawyer sniffin' about the place."

"You can bring your dog inside," Annabeth said cheerfully. "I'm sure Miranda won't hurt him. She's a very gentle animal."

Wiggins gaped at Miss Gentry. He didn't wish to be rude, but he certainly wasn't worried about that bloodhound hurting Fred. Fred could look after himself, thank you very much.

"That's very kind of you, Miss Gentry," Mrs. Jeffries said quickly. She could tell by the footman's expression that he was rather offended.

Upon hearing her name, Miranda trotted down the short hallway to the foyer. Fred's lip curled back, but he didn't growl. The bloodhound simply wagged her tail, looking for all the world like she wanted to be his friend. "Be nice, now, Fred," Wiggins chided the dog. Fred gave his tail one perfunctory wag and stared up at his master.

"Shall we move into the drawing room?" Annabeth said. "Martha's out visiting her young man's family, so I'm afraid it's just me and Miranda here."

"You're all alone?" Mrs. Jeffries didn't like the sound of that.

For a moment Annabeth was taken aback. "Oh dear, I see what you mean. That sounds rather foolish considering I came to you for help because someone was trying to kill me. But honestly, I'm not in the least nervous. Miranda's here with me. She can be quite ferocious if necessary." She patted her on the head and Miranda wagged her tail proudly.

"So can Fred," Wiggins put in. " 'E can be right nasty if I don't hold 'im back when 'e smells trouble." Annabeth smiled at Wiggins as they moved down the short hall and entered the drawing room.

Mrs. Jeffries sat down on the settee while Wiggins took the chair next to the door. Fred flopped onto the floor and stared at the bloodhound, who was now studiously ignoring him. "I know you're probably wondering why we've come," the house-keeper said.

"I rather thought you might have some progress to report," Annabeth said eagerly. She'd sat down on the love seat. Miranda curled up on the rug beside her and closed her eyes.

"We've made some progress," Mrs. Jeffries replied. "But that's not why we're here. Actually, we have it on good authority that Inspector Witherspoon will be here tomorrow to interview you about Stan McIntosh's murder."

"He's going to interview me?" Annabeth's eyes widened in shock. "Good gracious, why? I barely knew the man."

Miranda's head came up. Fred, seeing the other dog move, rose up to a sitting position.

"According to what I've learned, I think it's because someone told the inspector you'd had words with Mr. McIntosh." Mrs. Jeffries watched her carefully, wanting to see how she'd react.

Annabeth's brows came together. "Words? Well, I did get a bit annoyed with the man, but I'd hardly say we had 'words.' "

"Why'd you get angry at 'im, miss?" Wiggins asked. He didn't think Mrs. Jeffries would mind him asking a question or two. "If you don't mind me askin'."

"Because he told me to get off the school's property," she replied. "I didn't mind that so much. After all, that's his job.

What I got annoyed about was his refusal to even listen to me when I tried to explain why I was there."

"When was this?" Mrs. Jeffries asked.

Annabeth thought for a moment. "Oh dear, I suppose it was the day before he was killed."

Mrs. Jeffries carefully kept her expression blank. "Why, exactly, were you on the school grounds?"

"I wanted to have another look at the wall. I wanted to see the exact spot where those bricks had been loosened."

"Beggin' your pardon, miss," Wiggins said, "but didn't you tell us you'd been around and 'ad a look the day it 'appened?"

"Of course, but on the day it happened, I only had a rather cursory look at the wall. I wanted to have a good look this time."

"What were you hoping to see?" Mrs. Jeffries asked. Gracious, she had gotten off track, so to speak. But hearing Miss Gentry's account of what happened was quite interesting.

"I wanted to see if there were any marks along the top of the wall. So I took Miranda and we went around to the school. I slipped in through the gate and went around to the wall. We'd only been there a few moments when Stan McIntosh came charging out and ordered us off the property. I tried to explain, of course, but he was so rude." Her eyes flashed angrily as she recalled the incident. "He actually tried to grab my arm and drag me off the premises. Luckily, Miranda was having none of that. The moment he touched me she growled and bared her teeth. He let go quick enough then, I can tell you that. Of course, I didn't want Miranda to chew the man up, so I called her off and we left."

No one said anything when she'd finished. The only sound in the room was the click of nails against the wooden floor as Fred shifted positions. Finally, Mrs. Jeffries said, "I see."

Annabeth bit her lip. "Oh dear, do you think I ought to have mentioned this before. I didn't see that it was important. That's why I said nothing. I wasn't trying to hide anything. I was just so terribly worried about everything, you see. And no one, not even my own relatives, seemed to believe me."

"It's always best that we know everything," Mrs. Jeffries said softly. "Unfortunately, the incident was a bit more important than you think."

"Oh dear." Annabeth's brows drew together. "What should I tell him?"

"The truth," Mrs. Jeffries replied. "As a matter of fact, I think you ought to tell him everything."

"Everything? You mean about the attempts on my life and asking for your help —"

"Everything but that bit," Wiggins interjected. He glanced at Mrs. Jeffries. "I'm right, aren't I? She oughtn't to say anything about us being involved."

"That's right," the housekeeper replied. "Tell the inspector everything except the fact that we're involved. He doesn't know we . . . uh . . . well . . ."

"He doesn't know he has assistance on his cases from all of you." Annabeth laughed. "My lips are sealed, Mrs. Jeffries. I'll not say a word." Her smile faded abruptly. "That doesn't mean you'll stop trying to help me, does it? I'm sure your inspector is quite a nice man, but frankly, I've not much faith the police will be able to find the person who's doing this to me. They haven't found the person who killed that poor Mr. Porter."

"Don't worry. We'll still be on the case," Mrs. Jeffries assured her.

"Do you think my troubles are connected to McIntosh's murder?" Annabeth idly reached down and patted Miranda on the head. "I hope not. It's not quite fair, you know. I didn't really know him."

"Fair or not, Miss Gentry," Mrs. Jeffries replied, "there's a very good possibility your troubles and his murder are connected. In any case, it can't hurt to have the police asking a few questions." She almost mentioned that she thought the real connection was Tim Porter's murder, but she decided to keep that to herself for a bit longer. "By the way, what do you know about Phillip Eddington?"

"I don't know much about him at all," Annabeth said thoughtfully. "He seems a nice man. He's been a bit of an absent neighbor, I believe he travels a lot on business —" She was interrupted by knocking on the front door.

Miranda shot to her feet. So did Fred.

Annabeth got up, her expression puzzled. "Now, who can that be at this time of the evening?"

"Maybe it's Martha," Wiggins suggested. He reached down and took a firm grip on Fred's lead.

"Martha comes in the back door and she has her own key." She started for the hallway. Miranda trotted along at her heels.

"Do be careful, Miss Gentry. You don't know who is out there. Perhaps you ought to peek out the window before you open up," Mrs. Jeffries warned.

"Excellent idea." Annabeth stopped before she reached the door and hurried over to the front window, which looked out on the road. She pulled the curtains back. "It's the police."

"The police?" Alarmed, Mrs. Jeffries sprang to her feet. "Are you certain?"

"Oh yes; there's an older constable in uniform and another gentleman in plain clothes."

"Does he have a mustache and is he wearing a bowler hat?" She was already heading for the hall.

Annabeth dropped the curtain. "Yes. Is it your inspector?"

"Cor blimey." Wiggins jumped up and dashed after Mrs. Jeffries, who was now flying toward the back of the house.

"It's him all right," the housekeeper hissed over her shoulder. "If it's all the same to you, we'll go out the back door."

"I won't mention a word to your inspector about knowing you," she whispered loudly. She gave them a final wave and turned toward the front door.

Mrs. Jeffries, Wiggins, and Fred dashed

into the kitchen and hurried toward the back door. Grabbing the handle, she twisted and pulled the door open just as she heard a familiar voice coming from the front of the house.

By this time, Fred had gotten into the spirit of the game and fairly bounced along at Wiggins's heels. Until he heard that voice from the front. He skidded to a halt halfway through the back door. As Mrs. Jeffries was in the process of pulling it closed, she almost caught him dead center between the door and the frame. "Oh no, come along, Fred," she whispered urgently.

Fred, who was now very confused, tried backing up into the kitchen. "Come on, boy," Wiggins ordered. He reached down and grabbed the dog's collar.

But the house was small and the inspector's voice rang loud and clear in the quiet night.

"We're so sorry to disturb you, Miss Gentry," Witherspoon said. "But we'd like to ask you a few questions. Oh my, what a nice dog. Is it a bloodhound?"

Fred stiffened and tried to pull back into the house, toward the voice he knew and loved.

"Get him out, Wiggins," Mrs. Jeffries whispered. "We mustn't be found here."

"Come on, Fred," Wiggins hissed. He gave the collar another tug, but he didn't pull very hard. He didn't want to hurt the animal.

Confused, Fred looked back toward the sound of the inspector's voice then back at Wiggins. He barked softly. From down the hall, Miranda, hearing Fred, began to bark, too.

"Gracious," they heard the inspector say. "What's wrong with your dog? She seems most agitated."

Mrs. Jeffries leaned down, grabbed Fred's collar, and yanked him out the door.

From inside, Witherspoon looked curiously toward the kitchen. "I say, is everything all right? It sounds like there's something at the back of your house."

"It's cats, Inspector." Annabeth smiled up at him as she straightened up from petting her hound. "Miranda gets a bit agitated when she hears them."

"I could have sworn I heard a dog back there," Constable Barnes said.

"You probably did," Annabeth replied. "There's one or two strays in the neighborhood that like to chase the cats. Let's go into the drawing room, gentlemen. We might as well sit down."

Witherspoon and Barnes were soon seated in almost the exact same spots as Mrs. Jeffries and Wiggins had been a minute earlier. Barnes whipped open his little brown notebook and looked expectantly at the inspector.

"Do forgive us for coming so late, ma'am," Witherspoon said. "But we saw your lights on and thought that perhaps you wouldn't mind answering a few questions."

"About that poor man from next door?" She shook her head sympathetically. "He wasn't a very nice person, but he certainly didn't deserve to be murdered."

The inspector watched her carefully. "You knew Mr. McIntosh, then?"

"I didn't really know him, Inspector," she replied. "We'd met. But it wasn't a particularly pleasant meeting. As a matter of fact, I had words with him on the day before he died."

"Words, ma'am, you mean in the sense of an argument?" Barnes asked.

"Quite." She smiled at the constable and then patted Miranda on the head. "He chased me off the school's property and he wouldn't listen when I tried to tell him what I was doing there and why it was so important I have a look at the back wall."

Witherspoon sat up straighter. "Would you mind explaining yourself, ma'am?"

"Not at all, Inspector. There's a wall that separates my property from the school."

"Yes, ma'am, we know that. The uniformed officers did come around and ask you if you'd seen or heard anything unusual at the time of Mr. McIntosh's death."

Annabeth flushed in embarrassment. "I know. I ought to have told you about it then, but honestly, the police constable that came around asking questions was very rude."

"Rude, ma'am?" Witherspoon was genuinely surprised. The lads were trained to always be polite. Especially to women. "I'm sorry to hear that. I assure you, we'll look into it. Do please continue."

"As I said, there's a wall that separates my garden from the school. I'd gone over there to have a look at it and Mr. McIntosh caught me. He ordered me off the property. Apparently I didn't move as quickly as he wanted because he grabbed my arm and began physically shoving me toward the front gate. When he did that, Miranda raised a terrible fuss. She'd have gone for him if I hadn't called her off. McIntosh let me go and I left. That's all there was to it."

Witherspoon glanced at Barnes. Eddington hadn't mentioned the dog. "Why did you want to look at the wall? Is there some sort of property dispute?"

"Oh no, not at all. As a matter of fact, I rather liked having the school there. But I needed to look at the wall to see if there were any marks along the top where the bricks had come loose."

"I don't quite follow."

"Of course you don't." She smiled. "It doesn't make a lot of sense until you know the whole story. But you see, I wanted to see for myself if there was evidence that the bricks had been pried loose or if the assassin was clever enough to loosen them without leaving any marks."

Witherspoon gaped at her. "Assassin?"

"That's right. Someone is trying to kill me."

"Cor blimey, all of a sudden there 'e was, big as life at the front door. Mrs. Jeffries and I 'ad to scarper, that was for sure." Wiggins was once again telling the others about their close call. Now that they were safely back in the kitchen of Upper Edmonton Gardens, he thought the whole affair quite an adventure.

"Seems to me you two were lucky." Mrs.

Goodge clucked her tongue.

"Indeed we were," Mrs. Jeffries said. She cocked her head to one side and looked at Fred, who'd curled up on the floor beside Wiggins's chair. "We almost got caught because of Fred."

As if to apologize, Fred thumped his tail.

"But all's well that ends well," Wiggins said happily.

"Are you goin' to wait up for the inspector?" Betsy asked.

"Absolutely. I want to know what he thinks about the attempts on Annabeth Gentry's life."

"You think he'll take 'em seriously?" Smythe asked.

"Yes, I do." Mrs. Jeffries drummed her fingers lightly against the table. "At least I hope he'll take her seriously. It will make our task so much easier if he sees that there must be some connection between Stan McIntosh's murder and the attempts on Annabeth's life."

"Let's not be forgettin' the murder of Tim Porter," Wiggins put in. "Seems to me that's what started the whole mess."

Mrs. Jeffries frowned. "Oh dear, I didn't tell Miss Gentry to mention that fact to the inspector."

"You can do that if she forgets to mention it," Mrs. Goodge said easily. "Remember, her dog finding Porter's body was in the newspapers. Once her name is mentioned, you can tell him you read about it."

"You're right, of course."

"Seein' as we're all 'ere, I might as well tell ya what I found out this evenin'." Smythe kept his tone casual, but he was watching Betsy out of the corner of his eye.

"What do you mean?" Betsy cuffed him lightly on the arm. "Is that why you were so late getting home? You were supposed to be at the stables, not snooping about." She considered it most unfair that just because he was male he could go out investigating in the evenings, while she was stuck in the house until morning.

"I did go to Howards, but the stable lad 'ad already taken the horses for their run, and as I knew you weren't expectin' me back anytime soon . . ." He let his voice trail off.

"Oh, just tell us what you found out," Betsy said irritably.

He grinned. "I 'ad a bit of luck tonight. I went over to Miss Gentry's house on Forest Street just as the workmen were comin' out. I managed to strike up a conversation with one of 'em and we went to a pub. Not the one I'd gone to before," he added hastily. "Anyway, like I said, I got this bloke to talkin' and he gave me an earful about what's been goin' on at Miss Gentry's new 'ouse." He told them everything that he'd learned from Ned.

"So the workmen don't think the fire or the flood was an accident," Mrs. Jeffries mused.

"Ned's guv was certain the fire was deliberately started."

"But why?" Wiggins asked. "It don't make sense . . . if someone was tryin' to kill Miss Gentry, why try and burn down 'er 'ouse when she's not even in it?"

"Nothing about these cases makes sense," Betsy agreed. "Not yet, anyway. But they will. There's something here that connects everything. Something that we'll find if we just keep looking."

Mrs. Goodge looked skeptical. "I hope you're right. But for the life of me, I can't see what it could be."

"Good evening, sir," Mrs. Jeffries said cheerfully.

"Gracious, Mrs. Jeffries, you certainly didn't have to wait up for me," he said, handing her his hat. "It's terribly late. It must be after ten. You really ought to have retired for the evening."

"I'm not in the least tired, sir," she replied. But he looked exhausted. "Would you care for a cup of tea?"

"Not tonight," he replied. He headed for the staircase. "I'm quite tired. I believe I'll go right up."

"Are you sure, sir?" she hurried after him. "Perhaps you'd like some warm milk to help you fall asleep."

"Oh, I shan't have any trouble falling asleep tonight," Witherspoon called over his shoulder. "I shall see you in the morning."

Mrs. Jeffries gave in gracefully. The poor man was tired, so she'd let him have his rest. She checked that all the doors were locked and then she went up to her rooms. As was her custom, she didn't light the lamps, but instead went over to the window. In the darkness, she stared at the gas lamp across the road. The light glowed softly, casting pale shadows into the night. This was the strangest case. She was sure the murder of Stan McIntosh was connected to the attempts on Annabeth Gentry's life and Porter's murder. But how? That was the critical question.

She made a mental note to drop a hint to the inspector pointing out that the events must be connected. She frowned. If the inspector started asking questions about the Porter case, he'd draw Inspector Nivens's wrath. That was simply something they'd have to deal with if it happened. And what about the accidents at Annabeth's new home? Wiggins had made a good point. Annabeth hadn't been there when the fire and the flood happened, so one could safely say that neither incident was part of the continued attempt on her life. But what was the point if they were not accidents — if, instead, they were deliberate attempts to destroy the house? But why do that? Surely there was nothing hidden in the house. It had been empty since Mrs. Dempsey's death, six months ago. If there was something incriminating to someone in the house, there'd been ample time to get it out. Mrs. Jeffries sighed. Nothing made sense as yet. But she wasn't giving up. They'd find the connection. She was sure of it.

"Kippers, how delightful." The inspector sat down at the dining table and fluffed his serviette onto his lap. He picked up his knife and spread butter on the steaming fish on his plate.

Mrs. Jeffries poured him a cup of tea.

"Mrs. Goodge thought you'd need an especially good breakfast this morning. You had such a long day yesterday. Did you have a good meeting with the chief inspector?"

"I didn't meet with him at all." Witherspoon spiked a large piece of kipper with his fork. "He got called away at the last minute, so I went along and took a statement from Annabeth Gentry. She's the woman Mr. Eddington saw having words with Stan McIntosh shortly before McIntosh was murdered."

"Really, sir? How very interesting. Was she able to give you any useful information?"

Witherspoon swallowed his food and reached for his teacup. "Actually, it was quite extraordinary. She readily admitted to talking to McIntosh and, I might add, she claims she was handled most rudely by the fellow, then she told me she was a victim herself. She said someone's been trying to kill her for the past two weeks."

As Mrs. Jeffries wasn't supposed to know anything about Miss Gentry, she feigned surprise. "Goodness, sir, that is extraordinary. Did you believe her?"

"Well . . ." He looked doubtful. "I'm not sure what to believe. The way she described the attempts on her life could lead one to think she's simply imagining that a few accidents are really quite sinister attempts to kill her. Except for one thing. There have been some corresponding accidents at her new home, a home, by the way, that she's not even moved into as yet."

Mrs. Jeffries couldn't believe her ears. The inspector was willing to believe Annabeth Gentry because of the accidents at her house? "Goodness, sir, it sounds as if the poor woman has had a string of bad luck."

"Yes, extraordinary, isn't it. She had a flood and a fire in the new place." He waved a piece of toast for emphasis. "Mark my words, Mrs. Jeffries, something sinister is afoot. If it were simply those incidents which have happened to her, it would be one thing, but to also have the additional burden of having your home almost destroyed twice at the same time. Mark my words, something is terribly, terribly wrong. I'm determined to get to the bottom of it."

Mrs. Jeffries smiled politely. She'd have to bring another fact to his attention. She was sure Miss Gentry must have mentioned Miranda finding that corpse. It was a very pertinent fact. Surely the inspector would see the connection. Surely.

"And of course, the investigation on McIntosh isn't going all that well," he continued. "No one, not even the board of governors at the school, seems to know much about the fellow."

"Didn't the board get his references before they hired him?" Mrs. Jeffries pushed the extra serving of kippers closer to his plate. As long as she kept him eating, he'd talk.

"That's the odd thing, he wasn't hired by the board. He was hired by the headmaster. A Mr. Needs. We haven't been able to locate him."

"Do you know how long he worked for the school?"

He shrugged. "Two years. As to what he did before that, we've no idea. But we'll keep trying to find Mr. Needs and hope he can help with some answers."

"Absolutely, sir. It's just as you always say: when you're dealing with a murder, the first and best place to start is with the victim."

He blinked in surprise. "Er, yes, I suppose I did say that." Sometimes he couldn't remember all the things he'd said. Indeed, at times he was amazed by his own insight and intelligence. He certainly didn't feel very intelligent or perceptive. "But you know, Mrs. Jeffries, despite some of the things I say, when I'm working, I generally feel very muddled, as though I was trying to solve a murder using jumbled bits and pieces of information. It's most disconcerting."

Mrs. Jeffries suspected her employer was having grave doubts about his abilities. She was having none of that. "Nevertheless, sir. It doesn't matter how jumbled up the pieces are, you always end up putting them in order. It's simply what you do, sir. You catch killers."

Chapter 6

"This case is more twisted than a miner's whiskers. I can't make heads nor tails of it," Luty said. They were seated around the kitchen table at Upper Edmonton Gardens. Luty and Hatchet had been given a full report on everything that had transpired.

"This case might be complicated, but it's not impossible," Mrs. Goodge declared stoutly. "I think we're doing quite well. We've learned ever so much just in twenty-four hours and now we've got the inspector snooping about in Miss Gentry's troubles. Is he really going to interview her sisters and their husbands?"

"He has no choice," Mrs. Jeffries replied. "The inspector knows the motives behind most murders. Greed is number one, and now Miss Gentry has a fortune. She's no husband or children, so unless dictated otherwise by the terms of her will, her sisters get it all if she should die."

"And it looks like at least one of them could use the money." Mrs. Goodge sniffed disapprovingly. "According to the gossip I heard, the Cookseys' creditors are starting to be a bit heavy-handed. He's behind in his mortgage payments, and reverend or not, the building society wants their money."

Smythe started to open his mouth and then thought the better of it. He'd wait until after he spoke to Blimpey Groggins before he said anything.

"What were you going to say, Smythe?" Betsy asked with a smile.

He thought quickly. "Oh, I was just wonderin' when the inspector was goin' to interview Miss Gentry's sisters and their 'usbands? I'll bet they'll be surprised."

"No doubt," Mrs. Jeffries said. "But it must be done. Even if there is a connection between the attempts on Miss Gentry's life and the murders of Porter and Stan McIntosh, her sisters are, essentially, the only suspects. So far, they're the only ones who stand to benefit. No one appears to have had any reason to murder either Porter or McIntosh. At least, as far as we know at this point. In answer to your question, Smythe, I believe he's going to be seeing both sisters today."

"I'll keep a sharp eye out," Betsy said. "I'm going over to the Caraways' and the

Cookseys' neighborhoods today. I don't want to run into the inspector or Constable Barnes."

"I ought to have more information about their finances by our afternoon meetin'," Luty declared. "We know they're both pretty hard up, maybe by our meetin' we'll know if either of 'em are in hot enough financial water to commit murder."

"I thought I'd 'ave a snoop-about lookin' for information on McIntosh and Porter," Smythe said casually. He had only the barest twinge of conscience that he was going to be paying for the information. What was the point of having money if you couldn't do some good with it? "Maybe if I ask enough questions, we can suss out who wanted them two dead."

"I've got nuthin' to report," Wiggins said glumly.

"No luck finding any former pupils or staff from the school?" Mrs. Jeffries asked. She took a quick sip of tea.

"Not yet," Wiggins admitted. "But I'm not givin' up. I'll find someone who knows something."

"Of course you will," the cook assured him. She got up and began clearing the tea things. She didn't want to rush the others, but she did have people stopping by. The rag-and-bones man was going to be passing through about ten this morning and the boy from the greengrocer's up on the Shepherds Bush Road would be here with their order about ten-thirty.

"We'd best get started, then. We don't want to waste our day." Mrs. Jeffries rose to her feet. She could tell that Mrs. Goodge wanted her kitchen to herself.

"Will you be here today, Mrs. Jeffries?" Betsy asked.

"I'll be out for a while this morning," she replied. "But I ought to be back by early this afternoon. Why?"

"No reason." The maid shrugged. "I just wanted to be sure that someone would be here to help Mrs. Goodge with the tea. If it's all the same to you, I might be a bit late getting back today." She was determined to learn something useful. No matter how long she had to stay out.

"I ought to be home in plenty of time to help," the housekeeper assured her.

"You'll be 'ere for tea, won't you?" Smythe asked. He kept his tone casual, but they both knew he'd get worried if she was late.

"I'll be here," she promised him. "But you're not to get concerned if I'm a few minutes late."

"You do realize I don't have to speak to you at all." Elliot Caraway stared coldly at Witherspoon and Barnes. He was a short, pudgy man with wavy brown hair and a high forehead. He had a pencil-thin mustache, blue eyes, and looked to be in his mid-forties.

"That's not precisely true," the inspector replied. "Under the latest Judge's Rules, you do. However, you don't have to say anything that will incriminate yourself." Gracious, this man was a barrister. He really ought to be better versed in legal procedures.

They were in the drawing room of the Caraway home at number 11 Redden Hill Road. The house was a narrow two-story brick building with a tiny front garden. Though the place was in a decent neighborhood and certainly wasn't derelict, it had a faint air of benign neglect. The brown wool carpet was threadbare in spots, the rust-colored settee sagged ever so slightly, and the cream-and-brown flowered curtains were yellowed with age.

"You don't need to lecture me about the law, Inspector," Caraway snapped. He sat behind a desk at the far end of the room. He'd not asked the two policemen to sit down. "I know the Judge's Rules and I know precisely what my rights are. Please keep in mind that I'm speaking with you voluntarily and of my own free will. Now, please, get on with it. I've not got all day. I'm a busy man."

"Due in court today, sir?" Barnes asked politely. The constable had done some checking on Caraway. He knew the man hadn't seen the inside of a courtroom for three months.

Caraway sniffed disdainfully. "That's none of your concern, Constable! What is this all about?" He addressed his question to the inspector.

"It's about your sister-in-law, sir."

"My sister-in-law?"

"Your wife's sister, sir," Witherspoon said. "Miss Annabeth Gentry. Do you have any idea why someone would wish to do her harm?"

"Harm?" Caraway's brows drew together. "That's the most ridiculous thing I've ever heard. Why would anyone want to hurt her?"

"That's what we'd like to know." The inspector smiled slightly. "We have reason to believe there have been several attempts on her life."

"Attempts on her life," he scoffed. "Did

she tell you that? Gentleman, you're wasting your time on a fool's errand. Annabeth is cursed with a vivid imagination. It comes from having too much time on her hands. She should marry. Taking care of a husband would give her something useful to do with life."

"The incidents she described to us don't appear to be something she imagined, sir," the inspector replied. He didn't particularly like this man. He was rude, arrogant, and far too quick to dismiss the problems of others. He should have at least listened to them before passing judgment.

"What incidents? That nonsense about almost being hit by a carriage?"

"That and others, sir." Barnes was careful not to give out any details.

"I can't believe you're taking this seriously." Caraway leaned forward on his elbows and steepled his fingers together. The pose was supposed to make him look thoughtful. "If you'll forgive my being so blunt, Annabeth is prone to . . . well . . . shall we say she's a bit overly dramatic. As a matter of fact, my wife and I are seriously worried about her. She's not as strong as she appears to be."

"She seemed quite a fit and sensible woman, sir," Witherspoon said. "But we're not here to discuss the particulars of Miss Gentry's health. I understand you were present a few days ago at a tea party at Miss Gentry's, is that correct?"

Caraway straightened up in his chair. "We had tea with her last week."

"Did you have reason to go into the kitchen, sir?" Barnes asked softly.

"The kitchen?" Caraway looked puzzled by the question. "Of course not; why on earth would I?"

"The maid says she saw you coming out of the kitchen just after you and your wife arrived at the house," Barnes said. He looked up from his notebook.

"That's absurd — oh wait, I did pop into the kitchen for a moment. I, uh, needed to wash my hands. The water closet in the hall was occupied, so I went and used the sink in the kitchen. I'd quite forgotten."

As the constable had been bluffing about the maid seeing Caraway, he was quite pleased with himself. "When you were in the kitchen, did you happen to notice if there was a pot of cream on the table?"

"A pot of cream?" Caraway repeated. "I didn't notice, Constable. But I assume it's not unusual to find food in the kitchen. Look, this is a peculiar line of questioning. What's this all about?"

"Did you notice if the back door was open?" Witherspoon asked. Barnes's questions had gotten him into the spirit of the interview.

Caraway hesitated. "I don't think I remember — wait, I do recall. It was open. I remember because I looked out and noticed the table on the terrace had been set for tea. I was annoyed about that, because if we were going to have tea outside, it meant that Annabeth was going to let that wretched dog join us."

"You don't like the dog, sir?" Witherspoon prodded. He wasn't sure he trusted people that didn't like dogs. But, of course, he wouldn't let his personal feelings interfere with his investigation.

"I like Miranda well enough," Caraway replied. "But Annabeth's got the animal dreadfully spoiled. She claims the animal is trained. To hear her tell it, the dog can practically do anything except cook a five-course meal, but it's a lot of silly nonsense if you ask me."

"Bloodhounds are quite easily trained, sir," Barnes said. "The police use them often to do tracking."

"Naturally, I know that, Constable," Caraway said. "But Miranda isn't a properly trained hound. Annabeth's got some

171

absurd notions that she can train the dog on her own with hand gestures and bits of bacon. But it's all nonsense. Dogs are like women, sir, they need a firm hand and plenty of guidance."

"The dog did find a body," Witherspoon reminded him.

"Yes, well, even a broken clock is correct twice a day," Caraway sat back in his chair. "Inspector, are we almost finished?"

"Did you know a man named Stan McIntosh?" The inspector thought he'd toss that question in. One never knew what one would find out if one didn't ask.

"No. Is there any reason I should?"

"None at all, sir," Witherspoon said. "He worked at the school next door to Miss Gentry's."

Caraway stared at him blankly.

The inspector wondered if the chap ever read the newspapers. "Stan McIntosh was found murdered two days ago. I thought you might have read about it."

"I rarely read the gutter press, Inspector."

"It was in the *Times*," Witherspoon said. He decided to try a different tactic. "When will your wife be home, sir? We'd like a word with her as well."

"My wife? What do you want with her?

She knows nothing."

"She may know something. She does visit her sister, doesn't she?" Barnes said softly. "We'd be remiss in our duty if we didn't interview her."

"She'll be home this afternoon. But I shall insist on being present," Caraway warned.

"Why? Is there some reason you don't want your wife to speak with us alone?" The inspector surprised himself by the question. He'd no idea where it came from, it simply popped out. He generally wasn't quite this blunt with people. But the truth was, there was something about this fellow that put him off. The moment the thought entered his head, he was a little ashamed. An officer of the law oughtn't to let personal feelings dictate the way he asked questions. That was terribly prejudicial.

"Don't be absurd, man." A dull flush crept up Caraway's cheeks. "Of course there isn't any reason she oughtn't to speak with you. It's simply I don't want her upset, so I must insist on being present. You are suggesting, after all, that her sister's life is in danger." Glaring at them, he got to his feet. "Good day, gentlemen."

"It's all the same to me if you want to

buy me a cup of tea." The older woman stared at Wiggins suspiciously. But she sat down in the chair the footman had pulled out for her. "I'm in no 'urry to get 'ome."

Wiggins took a deep breath. He'd spent most of the day trying to find someone connected to Helmsley's Grammar School. He'd almost given up when the lad working at the greengrocer's had remembered that Stella Avery had once been a chairwoman at the school. Luckily for Wiggins, Stella still cleaned at a theater in Notting Hill Gate. He'd managed to find her just as she was leaving work for the day. "I'll get us some tea," he told her.

"And a biscuit," she ordered. "I'm 'ungry."

He took his time getting their tea and biscuits from the serving lady behind the counter. He was desperately trying to think of the best way to ask his questions. Stella Avery seemed a tad cranky.

He made his way toward the back of the small café. It was late afternoon and too early for the supper trade, so the place was empty. Stella Avery watched him out of sunken, brown eyes. Stringy strands of iron-gray hair poked out of the sides of her tattered bonnet, her complexion was sallow, and she was wearing a dingy, gray day dress that was badly wrinkled and had a button missing from the sleeve. She'd put her rolled-up apron on the table.

Wiggins put the tray down, served her, and then took a seat across from her. "I appreciate your agreein' to talk to me," he began.

"You said you'd pay me fer my trouble," she reminded him. "A shillin' and a cup of tea, that's what you said. I'll take it now, please."

Wiggins fumbled in the pocket of his shirt and pulled out the coin. " 'Ere ya are. Now, what can you tell me about Stan McIntosh?"

As he was paying for the information, he saw no reason to beat about the bush. He felt just a bit uncomfortable with the situation, he'd never paid someone to talk to him before, but it was the only way the woman had agreed to speak to him.

"What do ya want to know?" She picked up her tea and took a sip. "He was a pig of a man. I didn't like 'im much and neither did anyone else. What else ya want to know?"

He couldn't think of what to ask. So he asked the obvious. "Do you know of anyone who would want to kill 'im?"

She laughed, revealing a row of uneven,

rotten teeth. "Most of the pupils wouldna minded the old sod dyin', but I doubt they'd 'ave 'ad the nerve to kill the bastard."

"It couldn't be any of them. Why would they wait till now?" he mused. "The school's been closed for almost a term."

"It closed down at the end of Easter. Place was losin' money. Couldn't keep any students." She chewed her biscuit slowly.

"Did the staff dislike 'im, too?" Wiggins asked.

"Everyone disliked 'im but the head. He was always runnin' to 'im with tales about what everyone was doin'. Couldn't mind 'is own business if you know what I mean. 'E was such a nosey parker that one of the neighbors even 'ired McIntosh to keep an eye on 'is 'ouse when he was gone."

"Cor blimey, why'd 'e do that?"

" 'E didn't want to come back and find 'is furniture gone." She shrugged and took another gulp of tea. "What else ya want to know?"

Wiggins tried to think of more questions, but it was difficult. Generally, he had to be so careful when he was investigating that he didn't have time to actually think about what to ask; it was usually just keep them chatting and get what you could. "Did 'e ever 'ave any visitors or anythin' like that? Or did you ever see or 'ear of 'im goin' off and meetin' someone. What'd 'e do on 'is day out?"

" 'Ow should I know? I didn't live at the bleedin' place. I was just a cleaner."

Wiggins flushed. "Sorry. I guess I was just 'opin' you'd know a bit more. It's important, you see. This McIntosh fellow got 'imself murdered and the police ain't askin' the right questions. My guv wanted me to do some snoopin' about so's an innocent person don't get nicked for it." He crossed his fingers under the table as he told this lie and silently hoped the inspector would forgive him.

Stella's hard expression softened. "Who's yer guv?"

Wiggins was waiting for this one. "I'm not allowed to say, 'e don't want anyone knowin' 'e's lookin' into this murder." He glanced over his shoulder at the almost empty café and then leaned across the table. "I can tell ya this," he whispered. " 'E's someone known for wantin' justice. Someone who's not afraid to do a bit of lookin' on 'is own to make sure the innocent don't suffer."

"Are ya 'aving me on?" she demanded. But despite her harsh tone, she wanted to believe him. He could see it in her sad, tired eyes. She wanted to believe that somewhere out in what was for her a hard, cruel world, there really was a champion of justice.

A feeling of elation he'd never experienced before swept through him. He'd played about with a few of the details, but basically, he'd told the truth. He and others at Upper Edmonton Gardens were champions of justice. Maybe they didn't get their names in the newspapers and maybe they'd started their snooping because they were bored or they wanted to help their inspector, but now that they'd done it for a while, they were doing it for the best of reasons.

Justice. A commodity generally in short supply for people like Stella Avery. "Would I pay you for what you know if I was 'avin' you on?" he asked. "Stan McIntosh might 'ave been a right miserable person, but no one 'ad the right to kill 'im."

She hesitated briefly. "Well, bein' as you put it like that, I do sort of remember seein' some funny things goin' on a time or two."

"What kind of things?"

She glanced down at her empty cup. "Get me some more tea and I'll give ya what I know about old Stan."

"I'll get us both another cup." He picked up their cups and went to the counter. "Can we 'ave two more, please?"

"And some more biscuits," Stella called. "I want one of them kinds that's got chocolate on it."

"She's a right old tartar, she is," declared Eliza Adderly, maid to the Reverend Cooksey and his wife. "It's not that I mind hard work, I don't, but working for that woman is awful."

"Is she mean to you, then? Is that why you're going home?" Betsy glanced around the ladies' waiting room at St. Pancras station. She'd followed Eliza Adderly here and then struck up a conversation.

Eliza pursed her lips and shook her head. She was a tall, red-haired girl with a pale complexion and bright blue eyes. "It's my day out. I'm going to Little Chalfont to see my gran." She snorted. "If she'd had her way, I'd have had to be back tonight, but the reverend said I could stay over until tomorrow as I didn't get a day out last week. I'm only staying long enough to get a reference. Then I'm off."

Betsy tried to see the departure board through the window of the waiting room, but she was sitting at the wrong angle. "When's your train, then? I'm stuck here for a bit." She smiled and shrugged. "It's nice having some company."

Eliza laughed. "Oh, my train's not for another hour. I came early just so that I could get out of the house. Those two were getting ready to have another quarrel."

Betsy pretended to be shocked. "How awful for you. What a strange way for a vicar to behave. I always thought they were nice men."

"Those two go at it like cats and dogs." Eliza leaned forward eagerly. "Used to be they just fussed about money. About how it was all his fault they were destitute and about how she was always spending. But now they've got something even better to fight about. Mrs. Cooksey's sister inherited a fortune a few months ago and now they're always fighting over how they can get it away from her."

Betsy's jaw dropped and this time she wasn't pretending surprise. While she wasn't shocked that the good vicar and his wife were after Annabeth Gentry's fortune, she was amazed to learn they were stupid enough to discuss the matter in front of witnesses. "Gracious, they talk of such things in front of you?"

"Oh, they start out talking all quiet like, but before five minutes is gone they're screaming at each other like a couple of fishwives."

"That's terrible. How do they think they're going to get this poor woman's money?"

Eliza shrugged her thin shoulders. "First they tried to talk her into letting Reverend Cooksey handle it for her, to take over the investments and the business part. But Miss Gentry is a spinster lady and she's lived on her own a good long while. She told them both she'd handle her own affairs." Eliza laughed again. "They were both madder than wet cats when she wouldn't give in on that one. Then they said they thought it would be a good idea if they all moved into Miss Gentry's big house together . . . but Miss Gentry wasn't havin' that either and told them so straight out. There was a right old dustup about that one, I can tell you that. Mrs. Cooksey just about screamed her head off at her husband — said he'd jumped the gun and if he'd left things to her, they'd be sitting pretty now."

"What'd she mean by that?" Betsy didn't try to be cautious in her questioning. Eliza Adderly was a talker; either that, or life at the Cookseys was unimaginably lonely.

"She didn't say; about that time, Reverend Cooksey must have remembered I was in the house, too, because he told her to lower her voice. For once, she actually listened and did what he asked."

"Why are they so badly off?" Betsy asked. "You said he's a vicar."

"Oh, he is," Eliza replied. "But he's not got a parish. That's another thing they fight about. Accordin' to Mrs. Cooksey, that's all his fault, too. He used to be the vicar of St. Andrew's over in Clapham. But something happened and he and Mrs. Cooksey had to leave."

Betsy made a mental note to find out what had happened in Clapham. Vicars didn't just lose parishes like they lost buttons. There had to be a reason. "You poor dear, it must be awful for you, living in a house like that."

Eliza shrugged. "It's not for much longer. Like I say, I'm just stayin' long enough for a reference."

"Will they give you one?" Betsy asked. "Some people get right nasty when you give notice."

"They'll give me one, all right," Eliza said flatly. "If they don't, I'll go right to that nice Miss Gentry and tell her what they're plannin' on doin' next."

"This is goin' to cost you a pretty penny," Blimpey Groggins said bluntly. "It weren't easy findin' out about either man."

"If it'd been easy, I wouldn't 'ave 'ired you." Smythe shrugged. He wasn't concerned about the cost. Blimpey wasn't cheating him; it probably had cost the man a pretty penny. "Why was it so 'ard findin' out the goods on Porter? He was known to the police, 'e was a thief."

"Actually, the fellow was a pickpocket." Blimpey picked up his drink and took a sip. They were in the public bar of the Admiral Nelson. "Quite a good one, by all accounts."

"Then 'ow come 'e's dead?" Smythe asked. "Sounds to me like 'e picked the wrong pocket and got 'is throat slit for his trouble."

Blimpey frowned and shook his head. "I don't think so. Porter was a pro."

"Any idea on who might 'ave killed 'im?" Smythe knew that Blimpey's sources were likely to have far more information than they shared with the police.

"That's the funny part: no one knows. Word is that Porter made it a point to get along well with his . . . uh . . . associates.

Went out of his way to avoid makin' enemies."

"Maybe it was one of 'is marks that killed 'im," Smythe mused.

"It's possible, but not very likely." Blimpey took another sip. "Most marks don't even know they've been hit till they go to empty their pockets for bed. 'Course, there is one thing else — Porter had come into a bit of money. He was flashin' a wad of notes about two days before he died and he told one of his mates that there was more to come."

"Flashin' notes? From liftin' purses?" Smythe exclaimed. "Come on, pull the other one. No one's that bleedin' good." The good citizens of London had been contending with pickpockets since the Romans. Most of them never carried large amounts of cash on their person.

Blimpey hesitated.

"Go on, tell me. You must 'ave some idea what Porter was up to, and it weren't pickin' pockets."

"I don't want to set you on the wrong track," Blimpey said. "But it sounds to me like he was blackmailin' someone."

"You said Porter went out of his way to keep things nice and tranquil. Blackmail generally makes you a few enemies."

"That's one of the reasons I wasn't sure I ought to say anything. Blackmail would be out of character for Porter. But that doesn't mean he didn't do it."

"So what you're tellin' me is that it sounds like 'e was puttin' the screws to someone, but from what you've 'eard, Porter didn't generally have the guts to take on anyone who was likely to give 'im any grief."

"That's about the size of it." Blimpey waved at the barman. "You want another?"

Smythe shook his head. "I've 'ad enough, thanks. If Porter was blackmailin' someone, could you find out who?"

"My sources are workin' on that as we speak," Blimpey replied. "Mind you, that doesn't mean we'll find out anythin' worthwhile."

"Fair enough. Did you get anything on McIntosh?" Smythe took a quick sip from his beer.

Blimpey shrugged. "Not much. He worked as a caretaker at Helmsley's Grammar School for a couple of years. Before that, no one seems to have heard of him. But one rumor I got is that he was a seaman of some kind."

"Nobody 'as any idea why 'e was murdered?"

Perplexed, Blimpey shook his head. "Not yet. But I'm workin' on it."

"You don't 'ave much, do you?" Smythe muttered. He didn't really blame Blimpey. The man wasn't a miracle worker, but Smythe did hate having to go to this evening's meeting with so little information.

Blimpey's expression soured. "I ain't failed you yet, have I? Just give me a day or two and I'll know more about Stan McIntosh than his own mother."

"Don't be so bleedin' touchy," Smythe shot back. "You're the one that said this was goin' to cost me a pretty penny. You can't blame me for wantin' to get my money's worth."

"You'll get your money's worth," he promised. "Just give us a day or two."

"Fine, you've got it. Did you hear anything on that other matter?"

"Elliot Caraway?" Blimpey grinned. "Oh, I heard plenty about him. I was right, you know. He's about ready to be tossed out of his chambers. He's not had a brief in months and he's dead broke."

"What's he livin' on?"

"Credit, I expect." Blimpey shrugged. "Word I 'eard is that some relative of his wife's inherited a bundle and he's schemin' to get his hands on it."

"Could he do that?" Smythe asked curiously.

"When there's money involved, you can do all sorts of things. Mind you, with his skills in front of the bench, I don't think there's much chance he'd get a bloomin' cent out of her. It's been years since he won a case." He shrugged philosophically. "But that probably won't stop him from bringing the poor woman to court."

"On what grounds? You can't just go haulin' people into court willy-nilly. You've got to 'ave a reason."

"I don't know. You want me to find out?"

Smythe thought about it for a few seconds. He had no doubt it was Annabeth Gentry whom the barrister wanted to drag into court. He didn't think he needed Blimpey pursuing that line of inquiry. If a case was filed against Miss Gentry, they'd be the first to know. She'd tell them herself. "Nah, don't bother. What else 'ave you got for me?"

"Not much," Blimpey said. "I've still got my feelers out on that vicar and his wife. I'll let you know when I hear something, and as for that Phillip Eddington fellow, the only thing I could get on him was that he seems to travel out of the country a lot."

"Doing what?"

Blimpey grinned. "He goes off to Nova Scotia a time or two a year and does pretty much the same as you: he checks on his investments."

"You wanted to see me, sir?" Inspector Witherspoon stuck his head in Chief Inspector Barrows's office. "Oh sorry, sir. I didn't realize you had someone with you." He nodded politely to Nigel Nivens, who was sitting in a straight-backed chair opposite the chief's desk.

"Come in, Witherspoon." The chief waved him toward the empty chair next to Nivens. "Have a seat. This won't take a moment."

"Thank you, sir." He gave Nivens a friendly smile.

Stone-faced, Nivens stared back at him out of his cold, gray eyes. He was a portly, pale-skinned man with dirty blond hair worn straight back, a weak chin, and a large nose.

The inspector's smile faltered.

Chief Inspector Barrows cleared his throat. "Witherspoon, Inspector Nivens has brought it to my attention that you're asking questions about the Porter murder. Is that true?"

It took a moment before the inspector

realized what the chief was talking about. "Oh yes, but I'm not really asking questions about that murder; it's more along the lines of trying to find out if it has anything to do with another case I'm working on — the McIntosh murder."

"That's ridiculous," Nivens snapped. "There's no evidence that Stan McIntosh had anything to do with Tim Porter. Porter was a thief. That one is mine, so I'll thank you to keep your paws off it."

"If you don't mind," Barrows said sarcastically, "I'll handle this matter." He directed his words at Nivens. He didn't like the man. But Nivens had made a career of being politically well connected and the chief couldn't completely ignore his complaints. But no matter how many friends in high places that Nivens had, Barrows wasn't going to pull his best homicide detective off a case just because he might have stepped on Nivens's patch. Chief Inspector Barrows had no idea how someone like Gerald Witherspoon actually solved murders; all he knew was the man got results. That was all that mattered. "You say you were only asking questions about Porter in connection with the McIntosh murder?"

"Yes, sir. Well, there was another matter

that appeared to be connected. I was looking into that as well."

Barrows raised an eyebrow. "What other matter?"

"It was in my daily report, sir." Witherspoon pointed to a stack of papers on the side of the chief's desk. "I put it there this afternoon."

"Oh, uh, yes, well, I've not had time to read the dailies, so just tell me about it."

Nivens snorted faintly.

"It's one of our witnesses in the McIntosh case, sir. A neighbor to the victim. She was seen having words with the fellow on the day before he was killed. When I interviewed her, she claimed there'd been several attempts on her life."

"What's that got to do with Tim Porter?" Nivens asked harshly.

"The woman's name is Annabeth Gentry. Her bloodhound was the one that dug up Porter's body," Witherspoon explained. "So, of course, I began to suspect that it's all related somehow. Miss Gentry's dog finds a body; that's victim number one. Then there are attempts on her life, that's number two, and then, lo and behold, someone murders the caretaker next door. I mean, I don't think we're discussing a series of unrelated coincidences here.

There must be some connection."

"Rubbish," Nivens snapped. "I remember Annabeth Gentry. I interviewed her. She's a silly spinster who fancies her dog is smarter than most people. If someone was trying to kill her, why didn't she contact me? I'm the officer in charge of the Porter case."

Witherspoon had asked her that very question. She'd been quite blunt in her reply. She'd thought Inspector Nivens rude, bombastic, and worst of all, he'd not liked her dog. "I don't think Miss Gentry quite realizes there might be a connection between finding that body and the attempts on her life," he hedged. "As I was there to interview her about the McIntosh murder, she told me about the attempts on her own life."

"How many attempts?" Barrows asked.

"Three."

"All since she found the body?"

"Right."

Barrows nodded. "There's a connection. There has to be."

Witherspoon hesitated. "Well, there is something else you ought to know. Miss Gentry inherited a substantial amount of money recently."

"What's that got to do with anything?"

Nivens barked. "The attempts on her life are obviously tied to Tim Porter, so I should be taking over that investigation as well."

"Not so fast." Barrrows lifted his hand. "Witherspoon is right. If the woman received a large inheritance, she may have a whole passel of relatives trying to murder her. God knows that's happened often enough in the past. There might not be a connection to the Porter case at all."

"But, sir," Nivens protested, "how likely is that?"

Barrows shrugged. Things were getting very complicated. He wasn't even sure whether Witherspoon was defending his poking his nose into Nivens's case because there was a connection between the cases or because there wasn't. He didn't care, either. But he did care about catching killers. "We don't know. But I'm not taking him off the case. As a matter of fact, I'm beginning to think that maybe he ought to be investigating the Porter murder as well."

Nivens shot to his feet. "That's my case. You can't do that."

"But I can," Barrows said calmly. "You've had it for two weeks and you're no closer to an arrest than the day that dog dug up the corpse."

Chapter 7

"Who would like to go first?" Mrs. Jeffries asked.

Mrs. Goodge waved her hand. "Let me. My report is short. Truth is, I didn't have much luck today at all. The only thing I heard was that there was some foreign man who went to the Helmsley's Grammar School looking for his cousin. He was surprised it was empty and a school. Fellow kept insisting to the woman down at the post office that that was the address where he'd sent his letters." She waved her hands dismissively. "It isn't very useful, I know."

"What kind of foreigner?" Wiggins asked.

"What difference does it make?" the cook retorted. "It doesn't have anything to do with our case. According to Mrs. Pavel at the post office, it wasn't the first time some foreigner come in with the wrong address for a relative. But if you must know, he was an American or maybe a Canadian. They sound so much alike it's hard to be sure." She sighed loudly. "I know it's not much."

"Nonsense," Mrs. Jeffries said stoutly. "As we've found out before, everything is useful. We never know what detail will be the one that provides the vital clue for solving the case. Perhaps one of us ought to have a word with Mrs. Pavel. Who knows what we'll learn. I'm not sure what this means, but it could be significant."

"Can I go next?" Wiggins waved his hand in the air. "I found out a lot today."

Mrs. Jeffries glanced around the table. "As no one appears to object, go ahead."

He grinned and took a deep breath. "All right, then. I found a woman who used to clean at the school. She knew McIntosh. 'E wasn't much liked. Seems 'e liked runnin' to the 'eadmaster and tellin' on people."

"I'll bet the students hated that." Betsy laughed.

"Not just the students," Wiggins said. "The staff did, too. From what Stella told me, just about everyone 'ated the fellow. But I don't think any of them killed 'im. The school's been closed since spring term."

"Maybe someone was biding his time," Luty suggested. "I knew a miner once who waited twenty years to shoot the man who jumped his claim. Waited till the fellow was walkin' up the aisle of the church for his weddin' and then he shot him right in the back."

"Why'd he wait so long?" Betsy asked.

"He wanted to wait till the happiest day of the feller's life before he killed him, least that's what he said at his trial."

"I don't think McIntosh was killed on the happiest day of 'is life," Wiggins said with a frown. "From what Stella said, 'e was 'appiest when 'e was tellin' tales on someone."

"Did she know what McIntosh had done before he was the caretaker?" Hatchet asked.

"He worked at sea."

"Like a sailor?" Betsy asked.

" 'E weren't really a sailor, 'e worked for passenger liners. More like a porter or a steward. You know, fetchin' and carryin' and doin' for the passengers. But he stopped doin' that and got a job as the caretaker at the school."

"I wonder why he gave up the sea," Luty murmured. "Can you find out what passenger line he worked for?"

Wiggins nodded eagerly. "I expect I can. Stella give me the address of one of the cooks from the school. I'm 'aving a word with 'er tomorrow."

"You've learned a great deal, Wiggins," Mrs. Jeffries said. "Who would like to go next?"

"I might as well," Betsy volunteered. "I found that maid that worked for the Cookseys." She glanced at the cook. "The one you heard about."

"The one that was scared of her own shadow." Mrs. Goodge nodded.

"She didn't act scared when I was with her," Betsy said. "What's more, she was a real talker, too. I didn't even have to come up with any reason for asking so many questions." She told the others everything she'd learned from Eliza Adderly. "And when I asked her if they'd give her a reference," she finished, "Eliza told me they had to, that if they didn't, she'd go right to Miss Gentry and tell her what the Cookseys planned to do next." She took a quick sip of her tea.

"Don't stop now," Luty demanded. "Go on."

"That's just it," Betsy admitted glumly. "That's the one thing she didn't tell. Another girl from Eliza's village happened to come into the waiting room just then and I couldn't get anything more out of her."

"Maybe you can manage to run into her again," Luty suggested.

"I thought about that, but I don't think I can manage it. She wasn't sure which train she was taking back and I can't spend my whole day hanging about the St. Pancras station." Betsy wanted to get over to Clapham and pay a visit to St. Andrew's. She wasn't going to waste her precious investigating hours waiting for Eliza Adderly to turn up. Especially since she thought the maid might have been exaggerating just a bit. But she didn't want to share this with the others. She might be wrong.

"But you've got to find out," Wiggins insisted. "It might be right important."

"Maybe you can manage to see her again after she's come back to the Cookseys'," Hatchet suggested. "From what we know of their financial circumstances, they don't have a large staff."

"They don't," Betsy agreed. "They used to have a cook but she quit last month. Now it's just Eliza."

"Then it would be my guess that this young lady does most of the errands for the household," Hatchet said.

"She does." Betsy brightened immediately. "I know because she was complaining about having to go to the fishmongers for Mrs. Cooksey before she left. She was afraid she'd get on the train smelling of

197

fish. I'll wait until early tomorrow morning and then have another try at it. If there's shopping to be done, she'll be doing it then."

"Can I go now?" Smythe asked. He had a lot of information to share with the others.

"By all means," Mrs. Jeffries replied.

He told them what he'd learned from Blimpey Groggins without, of course, mentioning where he'd got the information. "So you see, not even the street toughs 'ave any idea who killed Porter."

"Is your . . . er . . . source a reliable one?" Mrs. Jeffries hated to ask such a question, but it was necessary. "Oh dear, that sounds awful."

"No offense taken." The coachman grinned broadly. "I know what you're askin'. Take my word, the source is a good one. If 'e says no one on the streets knows anythin' about this murder, it's the truth."

Luty frowned in confusion. "The one thing I don't understand is why your source thinks Porter was blackmailing someone. There's lots of other ways to get a wad of bills —"

"I know," Smythe interrupted. "My source weren't sure, 'e were only tossing the idea out because it seemed to be the only one that fit. But you're right, there's lots of ways to get money."

"But Porter is alleged to have said there was more coming," Hatchet reminded them, "and that implies that he had access to a steady source of cash. He wouldn't have made such a statement if he'd been referring to robbery or pickpocketing. The first is too risky and the second is too unreliable."

"So what we know is that no one knows why Tim Porter was murdered and there is some evidence he was also a blackmailer," Mrs. Jeffries said.

Smythe nodded. "That's about it. I've got my sources workin' on who Porter's victim might 'ave been."

"Maybe it was Stan McIntosh," Luty ventured.

"Now, madam, let's not jump to conclusions. We've no evidence the two men even knew one another," Hatchet warned.

"I know that," Luty replied. "But it would sure make this case easier if that was so."

"But even if it were McIntosh that murdered Porter, we'd still have the problem of who killed McIntosh," Mrs. Goodge said. "And so far, we've no idea."

"But we will," Mrs. Jeffries said firmly.

"No matter how complicated this case gets, we'll keep digging until we find the truth."

Inspector Witherspoon smiled gratefully as he accepted the glass of sherry. "Thank you, Mrs. Jeffries."

"You look like you've had a very tiring day, sir," she said, taking her usual seat.

"Indeed it was, Mrs. Jeffries. I must say, it wasn't too awful until right at the very end. There was a bit of a scene in the chief inspector's office."

Alarmed, she stared at him. "A scene, sir?"

"I'm afraid so." He sighed and took a sip of his sherry. "Inspector Nivens seemed to feel I was trespassing on his case. I don't know how he found out so quickly, but he'd heard I was asking questions about the Porter murder. He wasn't pleased."

"I'm sure he wasn't, sir," she replied. Nivens had probably had an apoplectic fit.

"Luckily, the chief understood my reasoning, you know, about the cases being related."

Mrs. Jeffries wondered precisely how the inspector had explained the connection. "You told him about Miss Gentry?"

"Of course. Well, I think Miss Gentry's

case is connected —" He broke off and frowned. "I mean . . . oh drat. I'm not sure what I mean anymore. But somehow, I believe that Miss Gentry being threatened is connected to McIntosh's death. It seems to me those threats must be somehow connected to her dog finding that pickpocket's body. Oh dear, you see how confusing it's becoming. But luckily, the chief quite understood." He took another quick gulp of sherry. "Unfortunately, Inspector Nivens didn't quite see the situation in the same light. He was rather unhappy with me. I was going to offer to share any information I received with him, about the Porter matter, but for some odd reason, the chief decided it would be best if I took a hand in that investigation as well."

"I think that's a jolly good idea, sir." She fought hard to keep her expression neutral. It wouldn't do to let him see she was elated at the thought of Nivens being out in the cold.

"I'm flattered by your faith in me, Mrs. Jeffries." Witherspoon sighed again. "But I'm not sure it's justified. I've no idea what to do next. Even with the new information I received from Inspector Nivens, it's all still so muddled and confusing."

Mrs. Jeffries knew his confidence was

slipping. She had no doubt that this was due to the confrontation with Inspector Nivens. Witherspoon was no coward, but he hated doing anything underhanded or unfair. She was quite certain that Nivens, knowing Inspector Witherspoon's good character as he did, had taken very unfair advantage of the situation and made all sorts of ridiculous allegations. "It might be muddled, sir, but you'll soon sort it out. You always do."

"In the past I have." He drained his glass. "But as Inspector Nivens pointed out, one can't be right all the time. I'm bound to fail eventually."

"Nonsense," Mrs. Jeffries said briskly. She was furious, but she didn't allow it show. "You have a gift, sir. An inner voice that guides you. Of course you won't fail. I think it's quite unfair of Inspector Nivens to make you doubt yourself like this."

"Oh, now, we mustn't blame Inspector Nivens, he had good reason to be upset. He'd made some progress on the Porter case, and of course, it is still his case, so to speak."

"But he's not made enough progress, sir," Mrs. Jeffries said. Drat, the fool was still on the case. "Otherwise the chief wouldn't have asked you to lend a hand."

"I'm sure Inspector Nivens is doing his best. Perhaps he simply needs more time," Witherspoon replied. "As I said, he's made some progress on the case. He'd found out that Tim Porter hadn't been working his usual pickpocket routes."

"Where had he been?" Mrs. Jeffries asked.

Witherspoon frowned. "Inspector Nivens hadn't found that out. But he'd not been picking pockets, that was for certain. No one had seen him on the streets for a good week prior to his death."

"Inspector Nivens actually managed to determine the right time of death?"

"The body hadn't been in the ground more than a day before it was found." The inspector suppressed a shudder. "And taking that fact, along with witness statements of the last time Porter was seen, means it was easier to pinpoint the time of death."

"Pardon my saying so, sir. But if that's all Inspector Nivens found out in two weeks, it's not very good." She watched him closely as she spoke, hoping to tell by his expression if there was more to come.

"I know." He sighed again. "But perhaps it'll be the best anyone can do. There are some murders that can't be solved, Mrs. Jeffries."

"And there are plenty that can," she told him. "Anyway, sir, other than a rather dismal meeting with Inspector Nivens, how did your day go?"

He brightened a little. "Quite well, actually. I think we're making progress." He told her whom he'd interviewed, what they'd said, and more importantly, what was left unsaid. Mrs. Jeffries listened carefully. She took each and every fact and tucked it away in her mind. Despite her bravado with the inspector, she knew these murders were going to be difficult to solve.

But she refused to believe that it was going to be impossible.

"And, of course, when I went back to the Caraway house to interview Mrs. Caraway, she'd not come home yet. I'll have to try again tomorrow. I tell you, Mrs. Jeffries, it's shocking how little respect some people have for the police."

"Dreadfully shocking, sir," she agreed. She clucked her tongue in reproof. "And didn't you say that Elliot Caraway was a barrister?"

"Which means he ought to know better," Witherspoon replied.

Mrs. Jeffries wanted him to know that Caraway was in dire financial straits. Of course, she couldn't come right out and tell him. "I'm sure he does, sir. But it *is* a puzzle, isn't it. You'd think that as he's a barrister, he'd be more sympathetic to any officer of the court. But then again, perhaps he's not had much luck in front of the bench and he blames the police for his failures. You know what I mean, sir. Perhaps he's lost a number of criminal cases. Goodness, sir, how very odd . . . Porter was a criminal and Caraway is a barrister. Do you think it's possible they knew one another?" She hadn't meant to plant that particular seed, but now that she had, she decided perhaps she'd see what grew. Maybe there had been a connection between Porter and Caraway.

Witherspoon stared at her for a moment. "Why, Mrs. Jeffries, that's a wonderful idea. I'll certainly look into it right away."

She didn't want him thinking she was giving him "wonderful" ideas. That could lead to all sorts of consequences. "It's very nice of you to say so, sir, but let's be honest here. We both know I was merely saying what you were already thinking —" She held up her hand as he opened his mouth to protest. "Now, now, sir, don't be so modest. Even if the thought wasn't precisely in your head the moment I spoke, you know good and well that by tomorrow morning you'd have been thinking along those lines. Just like you'll be thinking about how important it is to find out what you can about Miss Gentry's relations. After all, sir, as you always say, there are many motives for murder, but the usual ones generally turn out to be correct."

He now looked positively puzzled. "Er, uh . . . yes, I suppose I do say that. Uh, I didn't, perchance, happen to mention what I meant when I said it, did I?"

Knowing she'd succeeded in getting him so muddled he wouldn't remember where any ideas had come from, she laughed. "You're so amusing, sir. I must say I think it's remarkable that you've still got your sense of humor after a hard day's work. You meant that in each and every murder, if one kept the most basic motives in mind, one could generally find the killer."

He smiled weakly, but his eyes were still confused. "Oh yes. Well, yes, of course."

"So in the case of the attempted murder of Miss Gentry, the first thing one would do is find out who benefited from her death and, equally important, what their financial circumstances are now. Am I correct, sir?"

He nodded. But he still looked a bit confused. Mrs. Jeffries wasn't one to waste an opportunity. The timing was perfect. This was her chance to let him know what they'd learned about these strange cases. The inspector was tired, confused, and slightly tipsy, as he had returned home with a very empty stomach and it was quite a large sherry she'd given him. She reached for his empty glass. "Let me get you another drink, sir. I think after today's events you could use one."

" 'Ere, let me 'elp with that," Smythe said from the open door of the inspector's bedroom early the next morning. The inspector had already left for the day.

Betsy looked up from the tangle of linens she'd just pulled off the double brass bed. "I'm just changing his sheets. It'll not take a minute."

He pushed into the room. "It'll go even faster with two of us doin' it. Don't look so surprised. I do know 'ow to make a bed." It bothered him that she worked so hard. He had enough money that she'd never have to turn her hand for the rest of her days if that's what she wanted. But they'd decided that neither of them was ready to give up their investigating and so they'd decided on a long engagement. He just hoped it wouldn't be too long. He loved the lass more than life itself.

Betsy laughed and slapped the neatly folded clean sheet onto the center of the mattress. "All right, then. Give us a hand." She unfolded the sheet, grabbed the edges, and gave it a good shake. She giggled at his efforts to grab the linen on his side.

He finally got his fingers on it. "Are you going to try making contact with Eliza Adderly this morning?"

She nodded. "Pull that end up tighter. I'll find Eliza. But now that I think about it, she might have just been talking. You know, trying to make herself sound important."

"Why do you say that?" He tucked his edge of the sheet under the mattress.

She finished her side and then turned and picked up the clean top sheet she'd left on the chair by the window. "I don't know. The thought just suddenly occurred to me last night before I fell asleep. Once I'd thought of it, the surer I was that it might be true." Sometimes she didn't know how to explain things properly. She was sure there must be words that described what she'd felt, but she didn't know what they were.

"I know what ya mean." He grabbed the edge of the top sheet she tossed in his direction. "Sometimes the oddest things pop into my 'ead just before I'm noddin' off and it generally turns out to be right. But I still think ya ought to 'ave another word with the girl."

"I'm going to," Betsy assured him. She finished tucking the top sheet in and reached for the blanket. "Then I thought I'd pop over to Miss Gentry's neighborhood and see if anyone knows any more about the Caraways or the Cookseys." She frowned. "Seems strange to me that the only suspects we've got in this case is people that didn't even know the murder victim."

"You talkin' about McIntosh or Porter?"

"Either of them," she replied. "That's not right. Someone's got to know something about McIntosh. Everyone's got friends or relations somewhere."

"Maybe Wiggins will 'ave a bit of luck with the cook. Maybe she knew a thing or two more about the fellow." Smythe carefully spread his half of the blanket onto his side of the bed. "Actually, I was thinkin' of 'avin' a go at findin' out a bit more about Porter."

"Good." Betsy gave him one of her beautiful smiles. "He's a bit of a dark horse."

He didn't return it. He stared at her for a long moment.

Her smile faded. "What's wrong?"

"I'm wonderin' how long we ought to be engaged. You know how I feel about you, Betsy." He took care to enunciate his words properly, especially as he was talking to her. She'd never mentioned his lack of formal education or the way he spoke, but he knew she respected bettering yourself and he was determined to be everything she wanted in a man.

She'd been dreading this discussion. "And you know how I feel about you. I love you with all my heart. But I don't want to give up our investigating. Not yet."

"Maybe we wouldn't 'ave to . . ." His voice trailed off as he saw her shake her head.

"We would," she said fiercely. "Once we were married, you'd not be content for me to keep on being a maid. You'd want us to have our own home. Once we did that, we'd be gone and that would be it. You're a rich man" — she glanced up to make sure none of the others were passing by the open door — "and you'd not want me fetching and carrying for someone else, even our inspector."

What she said was true. He was rich and he did want to give her a home of her own. He wanted to give her everything. But he didn't want to give up their investigations any more than she did. He sighed. "All right, we'll wait. But not forever, lass. I do want to marry you."

"And I want to marry you," she said softly. "But we've plenty of time, Smythe. There's no rush." She didn't tell him she'd been giving their future a lot of thought. She realized something he didn't, or perhaps something he did, but wouldn't face.

She knew that no matter how big a house he bought her and no matter how much money he had, if they stayed in England, he'd always be a coachman and she'd always be a maid. But that was something they could talk about at another time. Right now she was glad she'd gotten him off the subject of setting a date for their wedding. Their investigations were too precious to give up yet. Being a part of them made her feel like she was contributing to something important. Something noble. She wasn't willing to give it up. Not even for love. Not yet.

Mrs. Goodge balled her hand into a fist, drew her arm back, and let fly with a punch. The dough crumpled on its side. She let fly with another punch and it flattened completely. "I did hear something this morning, but I don't think it's got naught to do with our case," she said casually. She wasn't sure the tidbit she'd heard was worth sharing with the others. Truth was, she'd been sorely disappointed in the bits and pieces she'd picked up.

"What's that?" Mrs. Jeffries prodded. She could see that the cook was in one of her dark moods. She sometimes got that way when she'd not had much luck with her sources. The housekeeper always tried to jolly her out of them. "Come now, Mrs. Goodge, do tell. I'm the only one here, so no matter how trivial you think it is, I'd like to hear it."

"Well . . ." The cook picked up a clean tea towel and draped it over the bowl of bread dough. "Mrs. Macklingberg, she used to do a bit of cleaning for that Mrs. Dempsey —"

"The Mrs. Dempsey that left Annabeth Gentry her house?"

"That's right. Michael, the butcher's boy, told me that Mrs. Macklingberg had told him that Mrs. Dempsey had gone a bit childish in her dotage."

"Childish how?"

"She'd started seeing things. She used to point at the mirror in the parlor and ask Mrs. Macklingberg to invite someone who

212

wasn't even there to tea."

"She saw people in the mirror that weren't there?" Mrs. Jeffries clarified. Unfortunately, Mrs. Goodge was right, this didn't have anything to do with their case. But she wasn't going to cut the cook short. She'd hear her out.

"Yes, poor old thing. It must have been awful for her. She saw men in the mirrors that weren't there and a few days before her death she'd started seeing monsters in the garden."

"How very sad." Mrs. Jeffries shook her head sympathetically. "I wonder what kind of creatures haunted the poor woman."

"Gargoyles." Mrs. Goodge shrugged. "Mrs. Macklingberg overheard her asking her neighbor if he'd seen the gargoyles digging out in the gardens. Eddington was quite polite about the whole thing; he very calmly replied that he'd only arrived home that very morning, so he couldn't have seen a thing."

"How awful to spend your last months on this earth with your mind going like that." She shuddered and sent up a silent prayer that God would take her fast, painlessly, and with all her faculties intact.

"It wasn't as bad as it could have been," the cook said. "She died very quickly after that."

"Old age does have some blessings." Mrs. Jeffries rose to her feet. She had a number of things to take care of this morning. "The body simply wears out."

"Let's hope our bodies go before our minds give out," the cook said. "I don't think I fancy people treating me as if I were a dim-witted child."

"Mr. Eddington, we came as soon as we got your message." Witherspoon smiled politely. He'd not planned on starting his day here, but when he'd got to the station, there'd been a message that Mr. Eddington might have more information for them. At this point in the investigation, Witherspoon would take any clues he could get.

Eddington gave a short, deprecating bark of a laugh. "Inspector, that's good of you, but it certainly isn't urgent. I don't even know if my information is useful in your investigation. Oh dear, where are my manners? You don't want to stand about out here on the doorstep. Do come in." He pulled the door wider and the inspector and Barnes stepped inside.

They followed him into the drawing room. He sat down on the settee and gestured for them to sit as well. As soon as they were settled, Barnes whipped out his notebook.

Witherspoon gave the man an encouraging smile. "Now, sir, what do you have for us?" He prayed it was something really useful. He didn't think he'd ever been this muddled on a case before.

Eddington looked embarrassed. "This is awkward, Inspector. Most awkward. But it's something I thought you ought to know. It's about Miss Gentry." He paused. "I don't think her dog really found that body."

Witherspoon blinked. "I assure you, sir, the dog did find a body. I checked."

He shook his head briskly. "Forgive me, Inspector. I'm not very good at explaining this. What I meant to say was that I think she may have known this Porter fellow before he died. Well, of course, if she did, then perhaps her dog finding the body wasn't as remarkable a feat as everyone thinks."

"Are you implying that Annabeth Gentry murdered Tim Porter?" Barnes asked. His expression was frankly skeptical.

Eddington looked pained. A slow, red flush crept up his cheeks. "I know it sounds awful and I've agonized over whether or not I ought to mention it. Miss Gentry seems a very nice woman. She took wonderful care of Mrs. Dempsey before she died. I honestly don't know what it means, sir. But I do know my duty and I finally realized I had to tell the truth."

"Exactly what is the truth?" Witherspoon asked.

Eddington took a deep breath. "I saw Annabeth Gentry giving a strange man money. They were standing in the churchyard. The next day, she and her dog found Porter's body. I think the man she was giving money to was Tim Porter."

Barnes looked up from his notebook. "Why do you think it was Porter?"

Eddington sighed. "I travel a lot, gentlemen. On business. Consequently, I tend to save my newspapers and read them when I get home. That's why I didn't come forward sooner." He reached for a newspaper on the top of the table next to the settee and waved it at the policemen. "I only read the newspaper account last night. It said Porter was wearing a gray workingman's shirt when he was dug up. The man Miss Gentry was giving money to in the churchyard had on that kind of shirt."

Witherspoon glanced at Barnes. The

constable's expression gave nothing away. "I see."

"I'm not accusing her of murder, Inspector," Eddington said quickly. "I almost decided to say nothing. But as I said, I know my duty. My conscience demanded that I tell you what I'd seen. This Porter sounds a disagreeable fellow, but he didn't deserve to be murdered in cold blood."

"I agree," Witherspoon replied. He gave himself a shake. By rights, he'd investigated enough murders that nothing ought to have surprised him. But this did. He simply couldn't think of what this new information might mean. Annabeth Gentry didn't seem like a murderer. For goodness' sakes, she had a dog. But he'd learned in the past that appearances could be deceptive. And even killers could have a dog. "What time of day was it that you saw Miss Gentry?"

"I'm not sure I remember the precise time." Eddington frowned thoughtfully. "Let me see, it was when I was out taking some air after breakfast. Yes, it must have been about ten o'clock."

"Did anyone else see Miss Gentry? Any of your servants or the gardener perhaps?" Witherspoon wanted as many witnesses as possible before he trotted over to Miss

Gentry's and began questioning her about Tim Porter.

"I do the gardening, Inspector," Eddington replied. "I enjoy it and it keeps one fit. As I said, I travel a great deal in my business. I only have an occasional cleaner come in, so there wasn't any staff to see Miss Gentry. Look, I've a great deal of admiration and respect for the woman. She spent an enormous amount of time with poor Mrs. Dempsey before she died. And I think it's tragic that now that she's inherited the house and Mrs. Dempsey's money, there's been so many awful things happening to prevent her from moving into her new home and enjoying it. I didn't tell you what I saw because I wished to slander the woman, but only because I thought it was my civic duty."

"We weren't doubting you, sir," Witherspoon said. "We merely wanted to get as much information as possible before we questioned Miss Gentry again. If someone else saw her with Porter, that would be most useful to know."

"You might ask the vicar," Eddington said. "When I turned around to go back inside a few moments later, I noticed he'd come into the churchyard."

"Was Miss Gentry still with Porter at

that point?" Barnes asked.

"I don't remember," Eddington admitted. "At the time, I thought nothing of the incident."

Witherspoon thought that odd. "Why not, sir? Surely a respectable woman handing money to a disreputable man is something that one doesn't see every day."

"I thought she was paying someone to work on the house," Eddington explained. "She'd hired some of the workmen herself, you know."

"She didn't employ a builder?"

"She did. But she'd also hired some laborers to do some of the unskilled work. At the time, that's what I thought she'd done."

Barnes looked up from his scribbling. "What kind of business are you in, sir?"

Eddington looked surprised. "Investments, sir. I find opportunities for a group of Canadian and American businessmen to invest their capital in. Why? Is it relevant?"

Barnes smiled. "No, sir. I was merely curious. I've always thought it would be nice to have a position where one could travel."

Witherspoon stared at the constable in surprise. Barnes was a homebody. He didn't even like the short train ride to Essex to visit his own relatives.

"Travel does broaden the mind," Eddington said. "But it also has some disadvantages. I won't have a wife to comfort me in my old age. I'm never in one place long enough to court a lady. More's the pity."

"Who are you?" The woman stuck her head out and glared at Wiggins with small, piggy eyes. "What da you want?"

He tried not to stare. She had the fattest face he'd ever seen. "I'm just wantin' to talk to you," he said. He held up a brown paper parcel. "I've brought you some buns. If you'll let me in, I'll share 'em with you." He thanked his lucky stars that Stella had warned him to bring food.

"You ain't said who you are?" She licked her lips as she stared at the parcel.

Wiggins didn't want to stand on the doorstep of the derelict row house a moment longer than necessary. "My name's Wiggins. Stella Avery sent me. She said you could 'elp me."

"Stella sent you?" The woman stepped back and pulled the door open. "Why didn't you say so? Come on in."

Wiggins stepped inside. The hallway was dim and smelled of boiled cabbage and rotting carpet.

"Close the door," she ordered.

He did as she instructed and hurried after her. She was the fattest woman he'd ever seen. The sides of her body brushed the walls as she waddled down the short hall. They came into a small, dismal sitting room. White curtains hung limply at the narrow window and the rose-colored settee was faded with age. A paint-splattered table and a spindly chair were the only other furniture in the room. Through an open door he could see one bare table and chair in the tiny kitchen.

"My name's Cora Babbel." She waved him toward the only chair. "Have a seat. Then tell us why you've come."

Swallowing hard, he sat down. "My name's Wiggins and Stella Avery said you might be able to 'elp me."

Her attention was fixed on the parcel. "Let's have them buns you promised," she said, reaching across the small space that separated them.

Wiggins handed them over. "Please, 'elp yourself." This was the most depressing place he'd ever seen and he'd been in some pretty awful places. He wondered how this woman managed to live.

"I've got a small pension," she suddenly announced. She unwrapped the parcel, tossing the string that held it together onto the floor.

Wiggins started in surprise. "How'd you know what I was thinkin'?"

She stared at him as she stuffed a bite of bun in her mouth. "Your face does your talking for you. What you was thinkin' was written as clear as the day is bright. Now, why'd Stella send you to me?"

Wiggins was glad she hadn't offered him one of the buns. "She said you might be able to tell me about Stan McIntosh."

"You with the police?"

"No."

"Then why'd you want to know about Stan?" She picked up the second bun and stuffed it in her mouth.

"Because I'm workin' for someone who's trying to catch 'is killer," Wiggins explained. He didn't think giving this woman the speech about justice for the common person would do much good. "And I'm bein' paid to ask questions."

"You're a private inquiry agent?" Her expression was skeptical.

He shook his head. "I'm just bein' paid to ask a few questions, that's all. You know anything about Stan or not?"

She laughed and reached for another bun. "Oh, I know plenty about old Stan. Plenty."

Chapter 8

Inspector Witherspoon wasn't certain what the proper etiquette was when someone deliberately kept the police waiting. As it was a lady, he didn't wish to be rude, but he didn't want the police to be made fools of either. He sighed inwardly as he glanced at Constable Barnes. "Do you think she'll be much longer?"

They were sitting in the Caraway drawing room. They'd been there for over twenty minutes and Mrs. Caraway still hadn't put in an appearance.

Barnes shrugged. "If she's not here soon, sir, we'd best go. There's a number of other people we've got to see today. We've still got the Cookseys to interview and you wanted to see Miss Gentry. Plus there's the former school secretary. He's supposed to have Stan McIntosh's references. I'd like to get a look at them, sir. We need to talk to someone who knew McIntosh."

"He is a bit of a mystery, isn't he?" Witherspoon said. "And of course, you're right. We do need to get cracking." He rose to his feet and started toward the hall, intending to call the maid and instruct her to have Mrs. Caraway come to the station. But he stopped abruptly and leapt to his left. A plump, blond whirlwind of a woman almost toppled him over as she charged into the room.

"What are you doing?" she demanded as she dodged to one side of Witherspoon. "Haven't you any manners? You almost knocked me over."

"I'm most dreadfully sorry," the inspector apologized quickly "I didn't expect you to come through the door so fast."

"It's my house, I can come through the door as fast as I please. I'm Ethel Caraway. I take it you're the police." She glanced at Barnes as she spoke.

"Correct, madam." Witherspoon moved back to the settee. "If you don't mind, we'd like to ask you a few questions."

"Of course I mind, but Elliot insisted I answer your questions. It is, of course, an utter waste of time." She didn't sit down; she simply crossed her arms over her chest and stared at them coldly.

"I believe, madam," the inspector said softly, "that we're the best judges of whether or not we're wasting time." He sincerely hoped that Ethel Caraway was wrong.

She snorted indelicately and walked to a chair. "Get on with it then." She sat down.

He wondered why she was being so very disagreeable. After all, it was her sister they were trying to help. "Mrs. Caraway, do you know a man by the name of Stan McIntosh?"

"Certainly not. Why would I? What's he got to do with Annabeth's tale of someone trying to kill her?"

"What makes you think that's why we're here?" Barnes asked.

"My husband. That's what he said you wanted," she retorted promptly.

Witherspoon realized this interview wasn't going at all well. She'd been rude, but he wanted to get as much information out of her as possible. "Mrs. Caraway, we're not here to inconvenience you. We've several very difficult cases and they might be related to one another. Your cooperation would be very helpful."

"I *am* cooperating," she replied. "But I don't see how Annabeth's wild stories have anything to do with that caretaker being killed."

"We've reason to believe there might be a connection," the inspector insisted softly. He didn't know why he felt that way, but all of a sudden he was absolutely certain that all of it was connected. The words of his housekeeper flooded into his mind. *You have a gift, sir,* she'd said. *You've an instinct for catching killers . . .* Well, he thought, perhaps that wasn't exactly what she'd said, but it had been something like that.

Barnes watched Ethel Caraway as Witherspoon spoke. Something flickered in her eyes, something that looked very much like fear. She knew something. The constable was sure of it.

"I don't know anything about Stan McIntosh and I've certainly no idea why anyone would want to kill him," she stated firmly.

"Have you ever been to the school?" The inspector had no idea where that question had come from; he'd simply opened his mouth and it had popped out.

"Certainly not," Mrs. Caraway replied. "That's the most preposterous thing I've ever heard. Why would I go to that tumbledown wreck of a school to see that disreputable-looking man —"

"How do you know he's disreputable looking?" Witherspoon asked.

"He's the caretaker," she cried. "Of course he's disreputable looking. He wears those filthy old clothes and doesn't cut his hair properly . . ." Her voice trailed off as she realized what she'd revealed.

"The only way you could know how his hair was cut, ma'am, was if you'd seen him," Barnes pointed out.

She recovered quickly. "You didn't ask if I'd seen him, Constable. You asked if I knew him. Of course I've seen him."

Witherspoon asked, "Where were you on Thursday morning?"

She was surprised by the question. "This past Thursday? I was at home."

"Was there anyone here with you?"

"I was alone, Inspector."

"What about your maid?" Witherspoon pressed.

She hesitated for the briefest of moments. "It was her day out," she finally said. "I've no idea what you're leading up to, but I assure you, I had nothing to do with the man's murder. Why would I want to kill a perfect stranger?"

"We're merely exploring possibilities, madam," he said quickly. "Have you ever heard of a man named Tim Porter?"

She frowned. "You mean the person Miranda dug up?"

"Yes, had you ever heard of him before your sister's dog . . . uh, dug him up."

"No. Why would I? From what I understand, he was a pickpocket. I don't generally consort with such persons."

"Excuse me, madam." The maid poked her head in the drawing room. "Miss Gentry is here. Shall I show her in?"

"Oh, it's all right." Annabeth Gentry popped into the room. "I'm family. Of course I can come in . . ." Her face broadened into a smile when she saw the inspector and Constable Barnes. "Goodness, how nice to see you again, Inspector, Constable."

Ethel Caraway closed her eyes briefly and sighed. "Annabeth, you really ought to wait to be announced. Even with family."

"Nonsense," Annabeth said cheerfully. "Can I bring Miranda in? I promise she'll behave. She's sitting right outside and you know how lonely she gets."

"Dogs don't belong in drawing rooms," Ethel Caraway retorted. Annabeth's face fell. "Oh, all right," she said, relenting, "bring the creature in, but mind that she behaves herself."

"She'll be good as gold." Annabeth hurried toward the door. "She's ever so well trained."

Ethel Caraway sighed. "We spoil Annabeth dreadfully. But that dog means the world to her. You don't mind, do you,

Inspector? Constable?"

Both men looked surprised to have been asked. Witherspoon spoke first. "Of course not, ma'am. We both like dogs. I've got one at home."

Annabeth swept back in with Miranda trotting by her side. The dog wasn't on a lead. But she stayed right next to her mistress. Annabeth took a chair to one side of her sister. "Sit," she instructed the dog.

Miranda sat.

"See, I told you she'd behave." Annabeth looked at the inspector as she spoke. "You'll appreciate this, as you've got an animal at home. But I've found the most wonderful way of training Miranda . . ."

Ethel Caraway sighed theatrically. "We know, dear. Come now, Annabeth, I'm sure the inspector and the constable aren't interested in your training methods."

"Actually," Barnes said, "I'd like to hear a bit more about them. The police use bloodhounds for tracking, sometimes —"

"Miranda would be a wonderful tracker," Annabeth exclaimed. She clasped her hands with excitement. "I've been working on teaching her to follow a trail. You know, laying down bits of food and then praising her when she —"

"Annabeth, please, the police are here to

talk to me. We need to get on with it." Ethel Caraway glared at her sister. "Now do let us continue."

"I'm sorry." She smiled apologetically. "I do get carried away."

The inspector suddenly had an idea. It would let him kill two birds with one stone, he somehow felt. He smiled at Miss Gentry. "I say, would you show us exactly where Miranda dug up Porter's body?" he asked.

"Of course," she replied, but her expression was puzzled. "I don't mind taking you there. But I didn't think it was important. That other police inspector said not to bother when I offered to show him."

"Excuse me, miss." Barnes frowned. "Are you saying that Inspector Nivens didn't view the body where it was actually found?"

"No, by the time he was on the case, they'd already taken the body away. He said he'd seen it and that where it was found wasn't important."

Barnes gaped at her as though he couldn't believe his ears. Even the inspector was stunned.

"But the surrounding area was searched?" Witherspoon pressed.

"Oh, I think the constables had a look."

Annabeth shrugged. "I don't really know. They bundled me off as soon as they got there. Why? Is it important?"

"Yes, Miss Gentry, it's very important." Witherspoon rose to his feet. He made a mental note to ask Miss Gentry about Eddington's report of seeing her in the churchyard, but for right now, getting to the scene where Porter's body was found was the most important order of the day.

"What's going on here?" Ethel Caraway demanded. "Are you finished with me?"

"For the moment, ma'am." Witherspoon turned his attention to Annabeth Gentry. "Are you free now? Can you show us where you found the body?"

Hatchet glanced over his shoulder and then climbed up on a carved gravestone next to the wall which separated the churchyard from the houses on Forest Street. He had a moment's guilt but he quickly squelched it. Since Mr. Edmund Pearsons had gone to meet his Maker over fifty years ago, Hatchet didn't see why the fellow should object to helping out a bit. After all, this was a murder investigation.

He stood on tiptoe and craned his neck to see over the top. He wasn't sure what he was looking for, but as his contribution to the case so far had been fairly limited, he was rather desperate to see something. All his other sources had dried up, and he couldn't get anyone new to talk to him, so he'd ended up here in the churchyard next to Annabeth Gentry's new home.

He could see the communal garden behind the two tall houses on Forest Street. The gardens had been terribly neglected. The grass was overgrown by a good three inches. The trees and hedges planted along the length of the back wall were wild and overgrown and didn't look like they'd been pruned since George III was on the throne.

From behind him, he heard the rustle of footsteps. "Excuse me, sir. May I be of some assistance?"

Hatchet whirled around. A short, rotund fellow dressed all in black smiled at him. It was the vicar. His bald head gleamed in the midday sun and his brown eyes twinkled merrily. "I'm Father Jerridan." The priest extended his hand.

"Good day, Father." Hatchet shook hands with him, realized he was still standing on the top of poor old Pearsons's monument, and leapt off. "Do please excuse me, I meant no disrespect to the grave. I was . . . curious about the garden next door, that's all."

"That's quite all right," the priest replied. "No need to apologize. Is there something I can help you with?"

"Yes, Father, there is." Hatchet hesitated, not certain of what to say to the vicar. He didn't want to lie to a man of the cloth, but he did want information. "Do you happen to know a Miss Annabeth Gentry?"

"I've met Miss Gentry," he replied. "Fine woman. She was engaged at one time to the son of one of our flock. Poor fellow died. Miss Gentry was very good to his mother. Mrs. Dempsey's last years were made far happier by the companionship she received from the woman who would have been her daughter-in-law." The priest's eyes narrowed suspiciously. "Tell me, sir, what's your interest in Miss Gentry?"

Hatchet wanted to be as truthful as possible, yet he also wanted to protect Miss Gentry from wagging tongues. "Lately Miss Gentry has been frightened by some very unfortunate incidents."

"Unfortunate incidents? What kind of incidents?"

"It's rather delicate, Father," Hatchet hedged. "I'm sure you understand. It's quite confidential."

"I'm a man of the cloth, sir. I know

how to hold my tongue."

"Let's just say she has reason to believe some individual may be trying to do her harm."

"You mean someone is threatening her?" The priest's bushy eyebrows rose. "Then you're a private inquiry agent? Oh dear, how very awful for Miss Gentry. As I said, she's a fine woman. Well, what can I tell you? Ask away. I'll do what I can to help."

"Thank you, sir." Hatchet gave him a grateful smile. "You'll be doing Miss Gentry a great service and I know I can trust your discretion in this matter." He had only the barest of qualms about questioning a priest under false pretenses. After all, catching a murderer was more important than correcting the erroneous impression that he was a private inquiry agent. Nevertheless, he resolved to put a couple of pounds in the church collection box. "Do you know of anyone who doesn't like Miss Gentry?"

"Oh, no, no, everyone around her quite admires and likes her. She's very kind. Well, perhaps I shouldn't say everyone, her brother-in-law is a bit of a bother, but I mustn't speak ill of a fellow priest."

"Her brother-in-law has been annoying her?" Hatchet pressed.

"No, no. He's only looking out for Miss Gentry's best interests. He'd never hurt her." The priest clamped his mouth and gave him a strained smile.

Hatchet knew he'd get nothing more from Father Jerridan about the Reverend Harold Cooksey. The priesthood didn't discuss one of their own to outsiders. But he wasn't going to let that stop him. "So there's no one who you know of that would wish Miss Gentry harm?"

"I don't wish to tell tales out of school, but I don't think her neighbor is all that fond of her." Father Jerridan jerked his ample chins in the direction of Forest Street. "She's not even moved in yet and they've had words."

"Words? You mean they've had an argument?"

"That's putting it a bit too strongly," he replied. "You know, I'm probably making a mountain out of a molehill. Perhaps I oughtn't to have said anything. It was such a minor incident."

Hatchet didn't want the good father to get tongue-tied at this point. "Please continue, it might be very important."

"Well . . ." He shrugged. "It's so silly I'm not sure I ought to repeat it. They've gotten along quite well since Mr. Eddington moved in two years ago. It isn't as if I really thought Mr. Eddington didn't like Miss Gentry. I just happened to overhear him asking her to please keep her dog on a lead when she came to inspect the work at the new house."

"Mr. Eddington doesn't like dogs?"

"That's what struck me as so odd about the request." He stroked his chin. "The only other time I saw the two of them together was right after Miss Gentry got the dog, about six months ago, just after Mrs. Dempsey had passed away. At that time, I rather got the impression Mr. Eddington was an animal lover. He seemed very fond of the dog then."

"Where were they when you saw them?" Hatchet asked.

"Right here." The father gestured at the churchyard. "Miss Gentry and Miranda were on their way over to Forest Street and Mr. Eddington was taking a shortcut through the churchyard to the road. They met right here in the middle."

"Shortcut?"

"Oh yes. There's a gate just over there that connects the two properties." Father Jerridan pointed farther down the wall. Sure enough, there was a slender, wrought-iron gate. "It's an ancient right-of-way between the properties. Very few people know about it. But some do. The residents of Forest Street have been trying to get the right-of-way revoked for the past couple of years. Well, Mr. Eddington has; he's not a member of our church. But Mrs. Dempsey refused. She used the gate every Sunday until her health gave out."

Hatchet silently apologized to Mr. Pearsons. If he'd been using his eyes properly, he needn't have trampled on the fellow's grave! "I take it Mr. Eddington didn't like people being able to cut across his property."

"But that's what's so silly about the fuss he's been making. The right-of-way doesn't go anywhere but to the communal garden on Forest Street. There's no right-of-way past the houses and onto Forest Street itself. It literally ends at the garden edge."

"In other words, the right-of-way only benefits the people who live on Forest Street," Hatchet clarified.

"That's right, and there's only three houses there."

"Then why was Mr. Eddington upset enough to try and get it revoked?"

"Oh, sometimes tramps use the side entryway to the church when the weather is bad. They sleep there because it's partly enclosed and it provides a bit of protection from the wet. They're not supposed to, of course. But frankly" — he flushed slightly — "I look the other way. Our Lord did tell us that what we did to the least of our brothers, we did to him."

"Why would Mr. Eddington object to anyone sleeping there? You said he wasn't a member of your church, so why would he care?"

"The side entry is just opposite the gate. You can see right through to the gardens if you've a mind to." Father Jerridan sighed. "I'd thought he'd let the issue go, but a few weeks back, Mr. Eddington spotted another fellow having a sleep there, so I expect he'll be worrying Miss Gentry to get the right-of-way revoked again. I don't know why it bothers the fellow so much; he's not even here most of the time. He travels quite a bit on business. But perhaps that's one of the reasons he values his privacy. He does seem to come and go at the oddest times."

Hatchet nodded. "Did Miss Gentry agree to his request?"

"She said her dog was very well trained and that Mr. Eddington needn't worry." Father Jerridan looked troubled. "But I don't think he believed her. Mr. Eddington's face had gone red and he looked angry enough to pop."

"You saw him?" Hatchet asked.

The priest blushed. "Oh dear, I'm afraid I've been caught haven't I? Inadvertent eavesdropping is bad enough, but spying is even worse, isn't it?"

"Don't be so hard on yourself, Father," Hatchet said.

Father Jerridan glanced at his watch. "Oh dear, I must be running along, I'm going to be dreadfully late to the Ladies' Missionary Society meeting." He tossed Hatchet an apologetic smile and started toward the front gate.

Hatchet wasn't about to let him escape. "Father, wait. Can I walk with you? I've a few more questions to ask, if you don't mind."

"You'll have to hurry," the priest called over his shoulder as he reached the front gate. "Mrs. Vohinkle gets awfully annoyed if I'm late."

"We're not more than a quarter mile from your new home, are we?" Inspector Witherspoon said to Annabeth Gentry.

"It's over a mile if you go by the roads," she replied. "But if you use the footpath through there" — she pointed to her left, toward an empty field that opened up off a row of small houses — "it's a ten-minute walk."

They stood on the footpath that wound through open fields on the edge of Hammersmith. They were separated from the grim walls of Wormwood Scrubs Prison by a good half mile. In the distance, the whistle of a train chugging down the Great Western Railway Line shattered the silence.

Witherspoon glanced at Barnes, trying to read his expression. They were going to be stepping on some toes here. Searching a crime site that should have already been searched by another officer wouldn't make either of them popular with Inspector Nivens. If they found nothing, well, then perhaps Witherspoon would leave it out of his daily report. But he had a feeling they would find something.

He could have kicked himself for being so precipitous. But gracious, when he heard the site hadn't been thoroughly searched, he hadn't thought about the ramifications of dashing over here and doing the job properly. If Nivens got wind of it he wouldn't like it at all. He'd think it made him look incompetent and he'd strike back any way he could.

Witherspoon wasn't concerned for himself. But the constable didn't have a fortune. He relied on his salary to support his wife. The inspector knew he was a bit slow when it came to the internal politics of Scotland Yard, but even he understood that Inspector Nivens had enough friends in high places to do a lot of damage to a policeman's career. He would make a nasty enemy. "Er, Constable, if you'd like, Miss Gentry can show me the site and I can search it on my own . . ."

"Four eyes are better than two, sir," Barnes said calmly. "And we may have to do some digging. But I appreciate the thought, sir, and if I may say, sir, I, too, have a few friends at Whitehall."

Clearly confused, Miss Gentry glanced from one of them to another. But she was too polite to ask any questions. "It's just over there." She pointed at a spot up the footpath.

They followed her to a copse of trees and shrubs bordering the footpath. She and the dog led the way in amongst the trees. Once inside, tall brush grew up against the trees, making the area hidden and private. A perfect place to bury a body.

"It's just here." Miss Gentry stopped at

the edge of a circle of disturbed earth. There was still enough light to see the site clearly, and the actual spot where the body had been dug out was only partially filled in. They stared down at it.

Annabeth relaxed her hold on Miranda's lead and the dog edged closer and shoved her nose onto the ground. Keeping her head down, she sniffed her way around the circle.

"It's all right, girl." Miss Gentry called the dog back to her side. "She must still smell the corpse," she said.

Witherspoon was glad that his sense of smell wasn't as keen as the bloodhound's. He knelt down and studied the area. It looked like a hole filled with dirt.

Barnes walked to the other side and looked at Annabeth. "Exactly how was the body lying when you found him?"

She frowned slightly, as though she were trying to remember. "Well, let me see. I didn't get that good a look at it. Once Miranda started digging and I realized what it was, I dashed off to find a policeman. But I believe the head was at this end." She pointed to the closest edge of the hole. "Yes, that's right, because I remember seeing the man's hair. At first I thought it was some sort of animal, then I saw his hand."

"Right, then." Witherspoon took a deep breath and plunged his fingers into the damp soil. He began scooping earth out onto the perimeter.

"Exactly what is it you're looking for?" Miss Gentry asked.

"We're not sure," Barnes replied. He, too, was digging in the soil on his side of the makeshift grave. "Anything the victim may have had on him could have dropped under the body. When he was killed or when he was buried. We'll have to dig all this out."

"Can I help?" Annabeth asked.

"I don't think that would be a good idea," Witherspoon replied. "But thank you very much all the same."

Miranda watched them curiously. Suddenly she bounded over and began sniffing the dirt at the end of the grave where the feet would have been. She began pawing the spot.

"I think you ought to dig there," Annabeth said. "She's found something. Something that probably belonged to the dead man."

"How on earth could she do that?" Witherspoon asked curiously.

"She's a very smart dog," Annabeth replied. "She's still got the scent. There's something buried there, mark my words."

As the inspector's back was starting to hurt, he was willing to take the chance that the dog might actually be onto something. He shifted to the far end. "Can I have a look?" He gently shoved Miranda out of his way and began digging where the dog's nose had just been. For a few moments he found nothing, then his fingers brushed against metal. "I've got something." He got a grip on the object, brushed away more dirt, and yanked it out of the earth.

Barnes, Miss Gentry, and Miranda crowded around him to have a look, effectively blocking his light. "What is it, sir?" the constable asked.

Witherspoon held up a small, dirt-encrusted change purse. "It's a woman's purse," Miss Gentry exclaimed.

The inspector could see it was a purse, but that was all. "How can you tell it belongs to a woman?"

"Have a good look, sir." She bent closer and pointed to a spot right beneath the clasp. "It's made of blue velvet. I don't think there are many men who would carry a blue velvet coin purse."

"She's right, sir." Barnes squinted at the purse. "Why don't you open it."

"Good idea." He popped open the clasp

and looked inside the small bag. "There's nothing here but some coins . . ." He pulled out the biggest coin and stared at it. "It's not English." He held it up to get a better look. "It's a Canadian nickel . . . gracious, how extraordinary."

"What's the other one, sir?" Barnes asked.

"A penny. Canadian as well. Now, how on earth did Porter end up with a woman's purse and Canadian coins?"

"Looks to me like he was just doing his job. He was a pickpocket, sir" — Barnes rose to his feet and dusted off his knees — "and it looks like he picked a Canadian pocket right before he was killed."

Smythe couldn't believe his luck. She was going into a pub. He'd spotted the frizzy blond-haired woman when he was on his way down the Uxbridge Road. He'd recognized her as the woman who'd been sitting behind him at the White Hare Pub. She'd been talking about Stan McIntosh to her friend. He dodged around a fruit vendor pushing a handcart and across the narrow walkway to the pub.

It wasn't the nicest pub he'd been in, but it wasn't the worst either. There was sawdust on the floor, a sagging bar, and an empty fireplace. Most of the plain wooden tables were taken. The blonde was sitting hunched over a glass of gin by the one nearest the fireplace.

Smythe went to the bar and ordered a beer and a glass of gin. "Ta," he said to the barmaid when she slid the glasses in front of him. Tossing her some coins, he picked up the gin and headed for the blonde. "Mind if I join ya?" he asked.

She stared at him for a second before her gaze shifted to the gin in his right hand. "Not unless that gin's for me," she replied.

"It's for you." He slid the drink in front of her and sat down on the hard wooden stool. "I'd like to ask you a couple of questions if you don't mind."

She tossed back the gin. "You're the bloke that was at the White Hare the other night. The one askin' all them questions about Stan."

"I didn't ask all that many questions," he countered. "You lot closed ranks on me before I got my curiosity satisfied."

She laughed, revealing a set of yellowed, chipped teeth. "We weren't closin' ranks, man. Everyone was just scared, that's all. Last time anyone was in the pub talkin' about Stan McIntosh, he ended up dead."

246

"And who would that be?" Smythe asked innocently.

Her eyes narrowed shrewdly. "Oh, I think you know who I'm talkin' about all right, don't you, big fellow? Otherwise, you'd not be botherin' to ask questions. You with the police or are you one of them private inquiry agents?"

"Neither," he replied. He was getting a little confused. She seemed more than willing to talk and that made him uneasy. "I'm just a curious sort." He reached in his shirt pocket and pulled out a five-pound note. Her eyes widened. "If you answer my questions and tell me the truth, ya can 'ave this."

"Ask away, big fellow. My name's Emmy Flynt. What's yours?"

"Smythe," he replied. "Nice to meet ya, Emmy. Now, who was askin' questions about McIntosh that ended up dead?" He asked the question even though he knew the answer.

"Little sod named Tim Porter," she shot back, her gaze still on the note. "Pickpocket, he was. A little whiles back he come around askin' questions about Stan McIntosh; the next thing we 'eard was that some woman had found Porter's body over in them fields beyond Ellerelie Road.

Scared us it did. No one liked McIntosh. He was always a bit of a bad one."

Smythe nodded. He could understand why they'd kept quiet. They might have heard McIntosh was dead, but that didn't mean all his friends were, and to these people, crooks tended to run in packs. "So you knew 'im, did ya?"

"I worked in the laundry over at the grammar school before it closed. I met him there. Didn't like him much, no one did."

"What did you mean about McIntosh having money?"

"Huh?" She stared at him in confusion. "Whaddaya mean?"

"You said that old Stan could come up with a bit of the ready when he wanted to," he reminded her. "You said it to your friend that night at the White Hart. I 'eard ya."

She shrugged. "I didn't mean nuthin', I was just talkin'." She reached for the note.

Smythe snatched it out of reach. He knew she was lying. "Come on, now, what d'ya take me for? Tell me the truth and ya can 'ave the money."

Emmy worried her lower lip with her teeth, as though she were waging some awful internal battle with herself. "Oh, all right, then. But you're to keep what I tell ya to yourself. I've got a reputation in these parts and I aim to keep my name decent. Stan liked me. But I didn't like him all that much, if you get my meaning. He weren't overly fond of soap and water, you know. Puts a girl right off, that does. Anyway, the, uh . . . only way I'd have anything to do with him was if he paid me, you understand?" she finished belligerently. Then she looked away, unable to hold his gaze.

Smythe understood all right. She supplemented her income with a bit of prostitution. He didn't look down on her for it. He felt sorry for Emmy. You did what you had to do to survive. "I understand," he said softly, "and I'll keep my mouth shut. What else can you tell me about Stan McIntosh?"

"What do you want to know? I wasn't with him that often. But I know he's got plenty of money . . ."

"How do you know that?" Smythe asked. McIntosh flashing a bit of cash to pay for a woman was one thing, having a lot of money was a very different matter.

"Because he told me he did," she retorted. "He liked to talk a bit, did Stan. Especially afterward. He told me once the school closed and the place were sold, he'd be off to a life of luxury. Said he'd never have to fetch or carry for anyone again."

Smythe shook his head. "Was he just talkin', do ya think?" He didn't see how a few pounds in the bank made a fortune, and to anyone's knowledge, that was all McIntosh had.

"Nah, he was tellin' the truth. Stan was a talker but he wasn't a liar."

"Did 'e ever say where this money was?"

She shrugged. "Didn't ask, did I. Frankly, I didn't want to know too much about Stan McIntosh. Seemed healthier that way."

Chapter 9

It was quite late in the afternoon before everyone arrived back at Upper Edmonton Gardens for their daily meeting. Luty was fairly bursting with excitement, Wiggins's cheeks were pink, Hatchet's eyes sparkled, and Smythe looked like the cat that had just got the cream.

Mrs. Goodge and Betsy wore almost identical glum expressions. Apparently, it hadn't been a very good day for either of them.

"I don't think we've much time this evening," Mrs. Jeffries said without preamble. "So let's get right to it. I'd like to go first if no one objects." She paused for a brief moment and then continued. She held up a set of keys. The keys that Wiggins and Smythe had found on McIntosh's body. "I've been trying to think what we ought to do with these. I don't think they're particularly important evidence, but I do think the police ought to know about them."

"Cor blimey." Smythe made a face. "I can't believe we forgot about 'em. Maybe I ought to nip over and plant 'em some-where in the school."

"That's a good idea," she replied. "The inspector said the school was thoroughly searched, so I think our best course of action is to plant them on the grounds. Then we must make sure our inspector finds them. But for the life of me, I can't think of how we're going to do that without being too obvious."

"We'll find a way," Wiggins put in confidently. "We always do. Is that all you've got, Mrs. Jeffries?"

She had a great deal more, but she wasn't quite ready to share her ideas with the others yet. It was a bit too premature. "I'm finished. Would you care to go next?"

"I'd be right pleased." Wiggins told them about his visit with Cora Babbel. He was a true gentleman and he didn't mention her size. "She was the cook at Helmsley's Grammar until it closed. She had rooms on the far side of the kitchen. She said that Stan McIntosh was a right odd one and that no one at the school liked 'im."

"We know that already," Mrs. Goodge said irritably. She could tell the others all had plenty to report, while she had practically nothing.

"But what you don't know is that 'e used

to sneak out at night," Wiggins said. "Cora told me McIntosh would wait until the place were locked up tighter than a drum and then slip out the back door."

"Was he meeting a woman?" Smythe asked.

Wiggins shook his head. "No, that's what Cora thought at first. But one night she followed him. She was angry at him because he'd run to the headmaster with some tale about her stealing food from the school kitchen and sellin' it on the side."

"So she was trying to get the goods on him, was she?" Luty chuckled. "Good for her."

Wiggins grinned. "She didn't come out and admit it, but I think that's what she was doin'. Anyway, when she got outside, she saw it were a man McIntosh was meeting. The fellow was carrying something; Cora couldn't make out what it was, but it was something with a long handle, like a broom. They headed off toward the gate leading to the churchyard. Cora was goin' to follow 'em but she must've made some noise, because all of a sudden they stopped and turned in her direction. She had time to duck behind a bush, but it scared her, so when they went on, she went back inside."

"I wonder who it was he was meeting,"

Mrs. Jeffries murmured.

"I wonder what it was he was carrying," Hatchet added. "Somehow, I don't think it was a broom."

"What else has a long handle?" Betsy asked. She wanted to contribute something useful, even if it was just questions.

"Maybe he was meeting Tim Porter," Mrs. Goodge suggested. "Maybe that's the connection between Porter and McIntosh. They were up to something together."

"That's possible," Mrs. Jeffries murmured. "But if they were up to something together, what was it?"

"More importantly, who killed 'em?" Smythe said. He glanced at Betsy. Her brow was furrowed in concentration and he could almost see her mind working. He hoped she wasn't up to anything. There'd been a time or two in the past when she'd done things that put her in danger.

"Go on, Wiggins," Mrs. Jeffries ordered. "We're short on time here. The inspector might be home any minute."

"That's really about it," Wiggins said. "Cora didn't 'ave much else to say about Stan." He rather thought that McIntosh's night activities was an important clue. "The only other thing she mentioned was that he wouldn't let anyone else get the mail."

"What do you mean?" Hatchet asked. "How could he stop anyone from picking it up once it was shoved in the slot through the door."

"School had one of them locked baskets over their door slot," he explained. He referred to a square, woven metal device placed over the slot. It was hinged on one side and could be locked. "McIntosh kept the keys and he wouldn't let anyone, not even the head, 'ave 'em. Said unlockin' the basket and getting the mail was 'is job and 'is job alone."

"Hmmph," Mrs. Goodge snorted faintly. "Sounds like he put on airs."

"Is that it?" Mrs. Jeffries inquired. Wiggins nodded and she looked around the table. "Who'd like to be next?"

"I'll have a go," Luty said. "Stan McIntosh worked for Gibbens Steamship Lines. They go between here and Canada. Before that, he worked for the White Star Line on the North America run. He was a passenger steward up until two years ago. Then he suddenly up and quits."

"That must have been when he got the job at Helmsley's," Betsy said.

"It would 'ave been," Wiggins interjected. "Cora said McIntosh come to the place about then."

"Why would you give up a job traveling to go and be a caretaker at a school that was going broke?" Smythe asked. "I know stewards don't make a fortune, but that's got to be a better job than caretakin' at that ruddy school."

"Maybe he got tired of travelin' and wanted to settle down," Luty suggested. "Whatever it was, he quit and come to London. I also found out that no one knows anything about that Mr. Eddington. I asked my bankers and all my other sources in the City and no one's ever heard of Eddington or his investment group. I think that's mighty suspicious."

"Madam, many investors prefer to remain anonymous," Hatchet told her. "Besides, Mr. Eddington says his investors are Canadian and American. It's no wonder your sources haven't heard of them. They're foreigners."

"Seems like this case is filled with people no one's ever heard of," Betsy muttered. "Almost like they just popped up out of the earth."

"Is that it, Luty?" Mrs. Jeffries asked in an effort to hurry things along.

"That's all I have." She gave her butler a disgusted look. "Why don't we let Hatchet go next, looks to me like he's gonna pop a collar button if he don't get it out."

"Thank you, madam." Hatchet beamed at his employer. "If no one objects, I do have some interesting tidbits to share." He told them about his visit to St. Matthew's and his lucky meeting with Father Jerridan. He left out the part about masquerading as a private inquiry agent.

No one spoke when he'd finished. Finally, Mrs. Jeffries broke the silence. "I don't know what it means," she said, "but I'm sure it means something. But I don't think a minor dispute about Miss Gentry's dog being on a lead is really a good motive for attempted murder." But the moment the words were out of her mouth, something niggled at the back of her mind.

"Neither do I," Hatchet replied. "But so far, he's the only person we've found that has any reason to dislike Miss Gentry."

"But he doesn't have any connection with Porter or McIntosh," Mrs. Goodge put in, "so if he's the one trying to kill Miss Gentry, then her case doesn't have a thing to do with the other murders."

"I can't believe that's true," Mrs. Jeffries replied. The idea she'd just glimpsed had disappeared as quickly as it had come. She frowned slightly and resolved to try to get it back when she was alone in her rooms.

Smythe noticed the housekeeper's expression. "Are you all right, Mrs. Jeffries?"

She gave him an quick smile. "I'm fine; I was just thinking of something. But it wasn't important. Would you like to go next?"

Smythe nodded. He told them about his meeting with Emmy Flynt. He didn't mention her being a prostitute. "So it clears up why they all closed ranks on me at the White Hart that night. The last person who'd been in there askin' questions about McIntosh was Tim Porter and he ended up dead. They weren't coverin' somethin' up, they was scared."

"But by then they knew that McIntosh was dead," Luty pointed out. "So why was they scared?"

"They knew McIntosh was dead but they'd no idea who killed 'im; no one does. They'd assumed McIntosh might 'ave killed Porter because of 'is askin' all them questions about McIntosh. Then McIntosh 'imself was killed and none of 'em knew what to think except that there was someone out there killin' people left and right. Believe it or not, they was warnin' me, tryin' to do me a good turn."

"Did Emmy know how much money McIntosh had?" Betsy asked.

"No, but she was fairly sure 'e weren't lyin' to 'er about goin' off and livin' in luxury."

From upstairs, they heard the front door open. Mrs. Jeffries leapt to her feet. "Oh drat, that's probably the inspector. I hadn't expected him home so early."

"I'll get his tray ready." Mrs. Goodge dashed toward the wet larder. "Come on, Betsy, give me a hand."

"We'll meet back here tomorrow morning," Mrs. Jeffries called over her shoulder as she dashed for the stairs. "I have a feeling we'll have more information to share by then."

The inspector was in the drawing room by the time she arrived upstairs. "Good evening, sir. This is nice, you're home early."

"I'm going back out again," he replied. "Constable Barnes and I want to have a word with Reverend Cooksey and his wife. They don't live far from here."

"That's too bad, sir. You look as if you're tired. But Mrs. Goodge will have a tray ready in a few moments, sir. Would you like tea or sherry?"

"I'd love a sherry . . ." He hesitated. "But as I'm still on duty, as it were, I don't suppose I ought to. I've had the most bizarre day, Mrs. Jeffries." He told her about his rather unsatisfactory interview with Ethel Caraway and about going to search the spot where Tim Porter's body had been found.

"What did you do with the coin purse, sir?" Mrs. Jeffries asked curiously.

"Constable Barnes nipped down to the station and logged it in as evidence. I expect there will be some trouble about that. Inspector Nivens won't be pleased about our search."

"Then he should have searched it properly himself, sir," she retorted. She didn't think her inspector would hear one word from Nivens. Even he wasn't stupid enough to raise a fuss over evidence he'd have found if he'd been doing his duty. "So, sir, any ideas?"

"If you mean do I have any ideas about who the killer is or even whether or not the cases are connected, well, the answer has got to be no. I've not a clue." He sighed. "But I refuse to give up."

"That's the spirit, sir. Why, your tenacity has already paid off. You found that purse."

"Yes, but the purse may not have anything to do with Porter's murder. As Constable Barnes pointed out, Tim Porter was a pickpocket. He'd probably pinched the purse before he was killed."

"Excuse me, sir. If I remember correctly, don't pickpockets get rid of the purse as soon as they take the money out? Aren't they afraid of getting caught with an item that's so easy to identify?" She could hardly mention that her sources had made it clear that Porter hadn't been picking pockets on the day he'd been killed.

Witherspoon's brows drew together. "Why, you're right. That means that unless the murder took place within minutes of his picking some Canadian woman's pocket, that purse is some sort of clue."

"Now you just have to figure out what kind of clue it is," she said cheerfully. "By the way, have you found out any more about Stan McIntosh's background? You didn't say if you'd met with the secretary of the board and got his references."

"Oh, drat. I do hope the secretary will forgive me; in the excitement of the search, I completely forgot I was supposed to meet with the man. I'll have to do it first thing tomorrow morning. Ah . . ." He cocked his ear toward the hall. "Is that my dinner coming up the stairs?"

Betsy popped her head into the drawing room. "I've got your tray, sir."

"Excellent." He got up and followed the maid to the dining room. Mrs. Jeffries followed a bit more slowly. She had much to think about.

The Reverend Harold Cooksey didn't look pleased to be disturbed. He was a tall, thin man with a ruddy complexion and wisps of gray hair circling his bald head. His thin lips pursed disapprovingly as he looked down his nose at the two policemen in his small drawing room. "I was just about to do evening prayers, sir," he said to Witherspoon. "This isn't at all convenient."

"We're sorry to interrupt your devotions, sir," the inspector replied, "but we've come around twice in the past two days and neither you nor your wife were at home. We have some questions we'd like you to answer."

"Oh, let's get it over with, Harold." Louisa Cooksey, an older, fatter, and rather meaner-looking version of Miss Gentry, glared at the two policemen. "It's only Annabeth's silly nonsense they want to talk about."

"We take Miss Gentry's problems quite seriously, I assure you," Witherspoon replied. He was amazed that the same family could produce three such different women. "Do either of you know of anyone who would wish to harm Miss Gentry?"

"Absolutely not," Louisa Cooksey replied. "Why would anyone wish to hurt her?"

"She imagines things," the reverend added. "We worry about her health, don't we, my dear?" He addressed the last part to his wife.

"Indeed we do," Mrs. Cooksey affirmed. "She's quite delicate, you know. She oughtn't to be living on her own."

"Do either of you know a man named Stan McIntosh?" Barnes asked. He didn't like these two.

"No," the reverend replied. "Is there any reason why we should?"

Barnes didn't answer; he looked at Mrs. Cooksey. "Ma'am?"

"I saw him a time or two," she admitted. "You are talking about the caretaker of that school, correct?"

"Yes, ma'am. You saw him? When?"

"Well, I guess it was the day that poor Miranda got so ill. I saw him going into the school just as we were passing by in a hansom. But that hardly counts, does it?"

"Was he carrying anything, ma'am?" Barnes persisted.

"Not that I remember," she said.

The inspector looked at Reverend Cooksey. "Have you ever met a man named Tim Porter?"

"Isn't that the fellow Miranda dug up?"

"Yes, did either you or your wife know him?" The inspector was fairly certain he knew how they'd answer, but one could never be sure until one asked.

Louisa Cooksey's eyes narrowed angrily. "He was a pickpocket, Inspector, hardly the sort of person we'd be acquainted with."

"We don't know the man," the reverend stated. "We never heard of him until all this fuss started. Look, Inspector, how much longer is this likely to take? I've an appointment this evening and I don't wish to be late."

Witherspoon glanced at Barnes. He snapped his notebook closed, a sure indication that he had no more questions to ask. The inspector couldn't think of anything else to ask them. Once again, it was a bit of a dead end. "I believe we're finished, sir. Oh, just one more thing. On the day you stopped by Miss Gentry's to have tea, the day Miranda took ill, did you happen to notice if the back door was open?"

Both the reverend and his wife answered at the same time.

"It was open," she said.

"Closed," he stated firmly.

Mrs. Jeffries waited up for the inspector, but it was so late by the time he returned home that she got only the barest details out of him about his visit with the Cookseys. She wished him a good night at the top of the staircase and went to her rooms.

She didn't bother to light the lamps. She wanted the darkness. She wanted to put her mind at ease and let the information they had gathered about his case flow about in her head until it made sense.

She sat down in her chair and closed her eyes. Then she forced her body to relax. Little by little, the bits and pieces began to coalesce and form themselves into the beginnings of a pattern. Porter was murdered first and then McIntosh. So she decided that she could safely assume that the same person killed them both. It was finding Porter's body that had involved Annabeth Gentry, so now the killer or killers were trying to murder her, but they wanted her murder to look like an accident. Why?

She sighed and opened her eyes. The pattern she'd thought was forming shifted suddenly in her head and now nothing made sense. Annabeth Gentry's death was supposed to look like an accident. That could only mean that whoever it was who was trying to kill her didn't want the police to investigate her death. And they wouldn't if the coroner ruled it was an accident.

Then why, she asked herself, hadn't the killer cared about the police investigating Porter and McIntosh's deaths? They might have been poor and had no family to raise a fuss — She stopped as the idea that had come to her earlier took root in her mind. The answer, she realized, was simple. The killer hadn't cared because there was nothing that could connect him or her with Porter and McIntosh. Those poor wretches had lived solitary lives, with virtually no connection to anyone or anything. How had Betsy put it? *As if they'd popped up on the face of the earth.* The police would do their best, but after a few weeks,. other cases would demand their attention and they'd certainly put these murders on the back burner. Neither man had anyone to look after his interests. No one really cared that they'd been killed.

But Annabeth Gentry was different. She had friends and relatives to demand that the police keep looking no matter how long it took. And the killer didn't want the police looking too closely into her death, because there was something in her life that connected her directly to the murderer. But what?

Mrs. Jeffries sighed and got up. She'd best get ready for bed. Maybe she'd think of something before she fell asleep.

Holding her shoes in one hand, Betsy tiptoed down the back stairs. If she was quick about this, she could get over to the school, have a look 'round, and be back in time for breakfast.

The floorboard on the bottom stepped creaked loudly. She stopped, cocked her head up the stairs, and listened for a moment. But she heard nothing. She continued on into the kitchen, put her shoes down on the chair, and then crept over to the pine sideboard. She'd seen Mrs. Jeffries put McIntosh's keys in the top drawer. She pulled it open and frowned. No keys. She pushed aside a ball of twine, a tin of sealing wax, and two rusted door hinges.

"Looking for these?" Smythe asked softly.

Betsy jumped and whirled around. Her beloved stood there, holding up McIntosh's key ring.

"What are you doing down here?" she snapped. "You scared me to death. Don't go sneaking up on a body like that, it's not healthy."

"More's the point, what are you doin' down 'ere at this 'our of the mornin'? And don't try tellin' me any tales, lass, you're fully dressed and wearin' your cloak, so I know you've taken it into yer 'ead to go out and 'ave a snoop on your own."

She debated arguing with him, but she didn't want to waste the time. "All right, what if I *was* going out? So what? It's morning. I can go out and do a bit of snooping on my own, I don't need your permission."

He glared at her. She raised her chin a notch and glared right back. Defeated because she wasn't in the least intimidated, he sighed. "I knew you were up to somethin'."

Betsy wasn't sure she liked that. "How?"

"Your face, lass. You were thinkin' about what you was goin' to do when we were 'avin' our meetin' yesterday. I could tell you were plottin' and schemin' about somethin'."

"I wasn't plotting anything," she retorted. "I was thinking we oughtn't to lose a perfectly good opportunity."

"To search the school ourselves," he said. "Yeah, the same thing crossed my mind."

She brightened immediately, delighted at the way their minds had come to the same conclusion. "Well, let's get moving, then. We've only got a couple of hours before the others get up."

He wanted to stay angry at her, wanted to give her a good talking-to about worrying him and trying to go off on her own. But the truth was, she looked so sweet and eager standing there with that shiny expression on her pretty face that he didn't have the heart to keep chewing on her. "All right, we'll go. But I want you to promise me you'll not do something this daft again."

Betsy was already grabbing her hat off the hat stand and heading for the back door. "It wasn't daft. You said so yourself."

"I said I 'ad the same idea to search the place, I didn't say it weren't daft to try and sneak off on your own." He was practically running to catch up with her. "And I want your promise, Betsy."

She gave in because she didn't want him nattering at her all the way to the school. "Oh, all right, I promise the next time I have an idea to go off, I'll tell you first."

She threw the latch on the back door and stepped outside.

Smythe pulled the door shut behind him as he followed. He wasn't sure, but he had the distinct impression he'd won that round far too easily.

Though it was early morning, the sun hadn't risen yet. They made their way to Holland Park Road and Smythe waved a hansom cab. He had the cab stop one street short of the grammar school. He'd learned to be cautious and there was no point in leaving a trail.

"We'll walk from 'ere," he told Betsy as he helped her down.

"Good idea," she agreed. Five minutes later, they were slipping through the heavy gates of the school.

"Let's go around to the back door," he whispered. Betsy nodded and they slipped around the side of the building. Smythe noticed that Betsy deliberately kept her gaze off the sheds. She'd not admit it in a million years, but he knew she was glad he'd come. In the dim light, this place was right scary.

Stan McIntosh's keys got them into the kitchen. The sun was just cresting the horizon, so there was enough light to get around without hurting themselves. The kitchen was huge. The floors were a gray slat, scratched and worn by years of shuffling feet. On the far wall were the sinks, greened with age and smelling of rotten vegetables. Above them, the wooden slats of the drying racks were broken and bent. Cobwebs hung from the ceiling, cupboards with doors askew lined the other wall, and a huge cooker, blackened with grim and soot, stood just the other side of the back door.

"McIntosh's rooms were supposedly off the kitchen," Smythe murmured. He noticed that Betsy hadn't left his side. As a matter of fact, if the lass got any closer, they'd be joined at the hip. "Come on, let's have a gander over 'ere." He started for the hallway opposite the cooker.

"But the police already searched his room," Betsy insisted. "I think we ought to have a good hunt around the school."

"All right, where would you hide something?" He swept his hands out in an arcing motion. "This place isn't exactly small."

"Well, we don't know that he had anything to hide," she replied. Drat, she hated it when he was right. The building was huge. It would take them hours to do a proper search.

"Then why the dickens are we 'ere?" He put his hands on his hips.

"Because he might have something here that'll give us a clue to this case," she shot back. "Oh, come on, you're right, let's start with his room. From what little we know of McIntosh, if he did have something to hide, he'd probably want to put it where he could keep an eye on it. His room's in the dry larder. That's what the inspector told Mrs. Jeffries."

They went down the short hall past the wet larder. Betsy wrinkled her nose. The wet larder smelled of rotten meat and boiled cabbage. She wondered how anyone could have stood living here. But sure enough, Stan McIntosh had turned the dry larder into his room.

"It's not much in the way of comfort," Smythe murmured. A simple iron bedstead covered with an ugly, green wool blanket and a pathetically small pillow was shoved up against one wall. A huge steamer trunk was at the foot of the bed and there was a small table and a chair in the far corner. There were no windows in the room.

"How'd he stand it?" Betsy asked. "The smell from the larder is enough to choke a horse. Why'd he stay down here? There must be dozens of bedrooms upstairs; why would he take this one?"

"Who knows? Maybe he didn't 'ave any choice."

"I don't believe that." Betsy stepped farther into the room. "He was here all alone, how would anyone know where he slept or what room he took for his own?"

"Come on, let's have a hunt." Smythe moved over to the bed, picked up the mattress, and peeked underneath.

Betsy did nothing; she simply stood where she was, shaking her head in consternation. "Look at this place. It's got dust everywhere —" She broke off as she realized the dust around the base of the trunk hadn't been disturbed. But the dust everywhere else in the room had. "Smythe," she said softly. "Let's have a go at the trunk."

Smythe cocked an eyebrow at her. "The police aren't stupid, lass. They'll have looked in there."

"I don't mean *in* the trunk, I mean under it." She rushed over and began pushing at the heavy thing.

" 'Ere, you'll 'urt yourself; let me." Smythe got on the other side and shoved it out of the way. He didn't know what his beloved expected to find. But he'd humor her. "See, there's nothing here. Just an empty floor."

But Betsy had dropped to her knees and practically had her nose to the floorboards. She pressed on one, then another and another. As she put pressure on one side of one of the boards, the back of it lifted. "See, the nails have been taken out of these." She gestured at the floor. "He's got something hidden here."

Smythe dropped down beside her. With his big hands and quick fingers, it took less than two minutes to pry half a dozen floorboards out of their way. They looked inside, but it was still far too dark to see anything. "Here goes." He plunged his hand down into the hole. "There's something 'ere." He grabbed what felt like a piece of carpet and pulled hard. But it was too big to come through. "Pull out some more boards," he ordered. But Betsy was already doing that.

"There, try it again," she said as she pried two more out.

This time it came up in a cloud of dust and dirt. Smythe sneezed and plopped it down on the floor by the truck. He brushed the dirt off the side. "It's a woman's carpetbag."

"An expensive one, too," Betsy said. "Come on, let's open it."

He brushed more dust off the thing and

popped the brass clasp at the top. The bag wasn't locked. It sprang open and they peeked inside. On the top was a flat leather case. "Let's have a look." Smythe took it out and flipped it open. A small, flat object that looked like a notebook fell out. He picked it up and studied it for a moment.

"Well, what is it?"

"It's a diary." He cocked his head and squinted at the fine print on the inside of the first page. "It belongs to a Miss Deborah Baker of Halifax, Nova Scotia."

Chapter 10

"I do wish you'd let me know what you were planning," Mrs. Jeffries said. There was just a hint of irritation in her tone. "If you had, we might have worked out some sort of plan. As it is now, we'll have to come up with a way to get this evidence to the inspector."

"I'm sorry, Mrs. Jeffries," Smythe said. "We shouldn't 'ave gone off like that —"

"It was my fault," Betsy interrupted. "All my fault. Smythe caught me trying to slip out early this morning and insisted on coming with me."

"It's no one's fault." The housekeeper laughed. Gracious, these two were adults. She had no right to berate them for taking a bit of initiative. "Forgive me, I have no right to chastise either of you for plunging ahead with the investigation. As a matter of fact, I should have thought to suggest we search the school well before this. However, we do need to come up with some way to get Inspector Witherspoon back to that room. Are you sure you put everything back in the hiding place?"

276

"We did," Smythe assured her. "We were right careful, too. After we'd had a good hunt through this woman's bag, I realized the best thing to do would be to let our inspector find it."

Mrs. Goodge put a fresh pot of tea on the table. "I still don't see what all the fuss is about. Who is this Deborah Baker anyway? How does she fit in with the whole mess, that's what I want to know."

"We don't know who she is," Mrs. Jeffries replied. "But I think it's important evidence. Betsy and Smythe also found a ticket stub from the passenger liner the *Laura Gibbens*. She's one of the Gibbens Steamship Line fleet and that's where McIntosh worked."

"All that proves is that McIntosh is a thief and that he stole some woman's carpetbag," the cook retorted. "I don't see how it has any bearing on our case." She gasped as Fred, his muzzle and paws covered with dirt, came trotting into the kitchen. "You wretched dog," she shrieked, "have you been out digging up my daffodil bulbs?"

Fred started guiltily and tried to slink under the table.

Wiggins leapt to his feet. "I'm sure 'e weren't botherin' your bulbs, Mrs.

Goodge. 'E's a good dog, 'e is. But I'll just run 'ave a quick look." He took off down the hall toward the garden. Fred, his ears pinned back, took off like a shot behind him.

"He better not have dug them up again," Mrs. Goodge muttered darkly. "That's twice I've planted them and I'm not goin' to do it a third time. I'll have his head."

"It's a dog's nature to dig, Mrs. Goodge," Smythe said helpfully.

The back door opened and then they heard, "You're a bad boy, Fred," Wiggins was scolding, "and you'd best go and apologize to Mrs. Goodge."

"Oh dear," Mrs. Jeffries said to the cook. "I do believe that Fred's in a bit of trouble. Why don't you plant the next batch in pots and put them up on the garden wall where Fred can't reach them."

Trying to control her temper, Mrs. Goodge took a long, deep breath. "I tell you, if he wasn't so handy in our investigations, I'd have that dog's hide." She was bluffing, of course. They all knew she was fond of Fred. He was getting a bit plump from all the treats she slipped him.

"Sorry, Mrs. Goodge," Wiggins said morosely as he and the dog returned. "It looks like he's done it again." This time, Fred did slink under the table.

"Oh bother, shouting at the stupid beast doesn't do any good." She gave a quick glare under the table. "Let's get on with our meeting. As I was saying, all finding that ticket stub proves is that McIntosh is a thief."

"That can't be it," Betsy said. "The sailing date on the ticket is from last year, and McIntosh wasn't working as a steward then. He'd been at Helmsley's for two years. So where did it come from?"

"And more importantly, where is Miss Baker?" Mrs. Jeffries muttered. She was staring at Fred's dusty paw prints on the kitchen floor. An idea was taking root in her mind, an idea that was so farfetched that it might possibly be true. But she needed a few more facts before she said anything. "For the time being, let's put the problem of the carpetbag to one side. There are one or two other matters we need to know before we can move ahead."

Smythe regarded her levelly. "You know who the killer is, don't you?"

"I have a theory," she admitted, "but I won't discuss it until I'm a bit more sure."

"Oh, come on, Mrs. Jeffries, give us a clue," Wiggins pleaded.

"I can't. Not until I know more. I could

so easily be wrong. I don't want to ruin our whole investigation at this point. If I am mistaken, it might completely fuzzy up our thinking and we'll never get this case solved." She got to her feet. "Luty and Hatchet will be here right after breakfast. I need to plant an idea or two in the inspector's mind before he goes out this morning. Then we'll get cracking. If I'm right, we've much to do and very little time to do it in."

She wasn't deliberately keeping them in suspense, but she was serious about not wanting to prejudice their thinking if she was wrong. She'd learned in the past that once a theory was advanced and acted on, it was difficult to let it go, even if it turned out to be wrong.

She left the others in the kitchen and took the inspector's breakfast tray up to the dining room. He was sitting down as she entered the room. "Good morning, sir. How are you?"

"Fine, thank you. Gracious, that smells delicious." He smiled approvingly as Mrs. Jeffries took the plate of fried eggs and bacon off the tray and placed it in front of him. She put his toast rack down next to his bread plate and then filled his cup with tea. "What's on your agenda today, sir?"

He sighed around a mouthful of egg. "I'm going to have another go at Miss Gentry. I completely forgot to ask her something rather important yesterday."

"And what was that, sir?" She poured herself a cup of tea and sat down next to the inspector. He hated eating alone.

"Just what I mentioned yesterday — that Mr. Eddington claimed he'd seen her giving money to some man in the churchyard. He thinks the man was probably Tim Porter."

"Yes, sir, you did mention that. Mr. Eddington seemed under the impression that the dog finding Porter's body wasn't accidental, right?"

Witherspoon nodded. "Honestly, I don't see how Miss Gentry could have murdered the fellow and carried him all that way up that footpath. I mean, can you see her humping along like some crippled monster, dragging a corpse and a shovel with her."

"Crippled monster?"

He laughed. "I'm sorry, I suddenly had this image of Miss Gentry with Porter's corpse thrown over one shoulder and a long-handled shovel over the other. Ridiculous, I know. Oh dear, you must think me monstrous myself that I can laugh at such a thing. Of course murder isn't funny."

"You're not at all monstrous. Sometimes the only way to keep the horror of something at bay is to laugh at it. I was wondering, sir, exactly what do you know about Mr. Eddington?"

Witherspoon took a sip of tea. "He travels a lot on business."

"Hmm, you mentioned that he doesn't have much staff in his home? That's odd, isn't it?"

"As I said, he's gone a great deal of the time."

"That's what I mean. From what you said about the homes on Forest Street, they're quite large. I should think he'd have someone looking in on his place from time to time. The way you described him, it's almost as if the man doesn't want anyone about the place."

"Perhaps he likes his privacy," Witherspoon murmured. But she could tell the idea of looking further into the background of Phillip Eddington was taking root.

"Oh, I'm sure he does, sir. I was just curious, that's all. As you always say, there's generally more to someone than meets the eyes. As a matter of fact, I happened to overhear some gossip about him the other day." She told him about Eddington's attempts to have the right-of-way revoked. "That is so strange, sir. Why should he care about some ancient right-of-way if he's gone so often?"

"Why indeed?" Witherspoon muttered.

"Does he have offices in the City?"

"No, uh, he doesn't," the inspector replied. "I do believe I ought to have another word with the fellow. Clear up a few bits and pieces. Perhaps I'll call round and see him after I've seen McIntosh's references and had word with Miss Gentry."

"That's probably quite a good idea, sir," she replied.

Mr. Malcolm Beadle stared at Witherspoon over the top of his spectacles. "I believe we had an appointment for four o'clock yesterday afternoon, sir." The secretary of the board of governors of Helmsley's Grammar School was not happy. His hazel eyes were cold and his thin lips pursed in disapproval. "I'm a busy man, sir. I do not appreciate having my time wasted."

They were in Beadle's book-lined study in St. John's Wood. Malcolm Beadle was sitting behind a huge, mahogany desk. Barnes and Witherspoon were standing in front of him like recalcitrant schoolboys.

Constable Barnes was getting annoyed. It was disgraceful how some people had such a lack of respect for the police. "We were called away on a matter of some urgency, sir," he replied before his superior could utter another apology. "The fact of the matter is, sir, police emergencies take precedence over appointments."

"But we are most dreadfully sorry," Witherspoon said for the third time. "We'll not take up much more of your morning. There's just one or two things we need." He frowned thoughtfully as the question he was going to ask flew right out of his head.

"May we sit down, sir?" Barnes asked.

"Hmmph," Beadle snorted, and jerked his head toward two chairs. "Sit down."

"Thank you." Barnes smiled slightly. "You said you'd provide us with a copy of Stan McIntosh's' references. Do you have it?"

Beadle picked up a piece of paper from off the desk and handed it toward the now sitting policemen. Barnes had to get up to reach it. "Thank you."

Witherspoon finally remembered what it was he was going to ask. "Is the school going to be sold soon?"

Beadle frowned, an act that brought his bushy brown eyesbrows almost together over his nose. "Sold? We've no intention of selling it, Inspector. Whatever gave you that idea?"

"Uh, one of the neighbors mentioned that Mr. McIntosh had said the school was to be sold. Perhaps he was mistaken."

"The property isn't being sold; it's being let and turned into a girls' school come the first of the year. McIntosh knew that. The new tenants had agreed to keep him on if he wanted to stay. He worked cheap and kept the windows from being broken by hooligans."

"Thank you, Mr. Beadle. You've been most helpful." Witherspoon rose to his feet. Constable Barnes stayed seated, his gaze on the paper in his hand. "Uh, Constable, perhaps we'd better go. We don't want to take up any more of Mr. Beadle's time."

Barnes handed the references to Witherspoon. "You'd better have a look at this before we go, sir. You may have a few more questions for Mr. Beadle."

Witherspoon scanned the sheet quickly. There were only four names on it. The last name was Phillip Eddington of number 1 Forest Street. "Good gracious. He never mentioned this."

"What is it?" Beadle asked.

"These names, sir, did you actually contact them before you hired McIntosh?"

"Of course; I wrote all of them personally. We wouldn't hire someone without checking references."

"Did Mr. Eddington reply to your inquiry?" Barnes asked.

"All of them replied. Otherwise we'd have not given McIntosh the position. Do you want to see the letters?"

"Indeed we do, sir," Witherspoon replied. "It's very important."

Luty shook her head in disbelief. "We should've searched that place way before this." She grinned at Betsy. "Smart girl. I wish I'da thought of it."

Betsy giggled. "Thanks, but it was really frightening. I'd have lost my nerve if Smythe hadn't been with me." She could admit it as he wasn't here at the moment. Mrs. Jeffries had sent him out on some mysterious errand.

"What should we do next?" Hatchet addressed the question to Mrs. Jeffries. But she didn't seem to hear him. She was staring at the wall with great concentration.

In truth, she wasn't listening. The idea that had come to her earlier simply wouldn't go away. But it was so bizarre. She was in a real quandary. She was sure she was right, but what if she was mistaken? Still, there couldn't be any other answer. Everything pointed in that one single direction.

Everything. The fire and flood at Miss Gentry's house on Forest Street, poor old Mrs. Dempsey seeing gargoyles in the garden, McIntosh sneaking out at night for secret meetings, the tramp sleeping in the church entryway, the entryway with a view of the communal gardens at Forest Street. No, she shook her head. It could only mean one thing. But how to prove it? That was the question. There was really only one way.

"Mrs. Jeffries," Hatchet said softly.

"Oh dear, I *am* sorry. What did you say?"

"I said, what do we do now?" He smiled at her. "You seem very lost in your thoughts. Is there something you'd like to share with us?"

"Mrs. Jeffries knows who the killer is," Betsy stated. "But she won't say yet."

"Only because I'm not completely certain. I do wish Smythe would come back. If what I think is true, then I'm fairly certain the information Smythe may come back with will prove it."

"We can be patient, Mrs. Jeffries," Hatchet said. "I say, Mrs. Goodge, may I have another one of your delicious buns?"

The cook shoved the plate toward him. "Help yourself." She was dying of curiosity.

" 'Ow long do we 'ave to wait?" Wiggins asked plaintively. He and Fred had kept a very low profile; they were both still in the doghouse over the daffodils.

"Not much longer, I hope."

From the street, they heard the distinct sounds of a carriage stopping in front of the house. "That sounds like Smythe now," Mrs. Jeffries said. Her spirits lifted enormously. "I told him to bring the carriage back with him. I expect we'll need it." She knew they would. She'd instructed him to bring the vehicle only if he was able to confirm what she suspected.

A few moments later, Smythe bounded into the kitchen. "You were right, Mrs. Jeffries, he's goin' to run. I followed him to Cook's. I overheard him buyin' tickets on the *Sarah Maine*; she sails at first tide tomorrow morning from Southampton." He flashed Betsy a quick smile and dropped into the chair next to her. "The 'ouse is up for sale as well, I spotted the sign in the front garden when I followed 'im home."

"Who we talkin' about here?" Luty demanded.

"I do believe it's time you shared your ideas with us, Mrs. Jeffries," Hatchet interjected. "Things appear to be getting very interesting."

"What's goin' on?" Mrs. Goodge asked. "Who's he been following all morning?"

"Cor blimey, Mrs. Jeffries, don't keep us in the dark," Wiggins complained. "We wants to 'elp."

Mrs. Jeffries held up her hand. "I'm sorry, I wasn't being deliberately mysterious. I asked Smythe to follow Phillip Eddington. I'm fairly certain he's our killer, but proving it is going to take a great deal of cleverness and luck. Now, we must act fast if we're going to keep him from leaving the country."

"Tell us what we need to do," Hatchet said.

"First of all," Mrs. Jeffries replied, "Smythe, you and Wiggins need to go get Miss Gentry. Tell her she must write the inspector a note that he is to meet her at Forest Street right away. She must tell him it's urgent. But you're not to bring the note here. Smythe, you take the note and find the inspector. Tell the inspector that Miss

Gentry brought the note here to the house and that she begged you to take it to him. Then be sure you tell him that as Luty and Hatchet were here, Hatchet and Wiggins insisted on accompanying Miss Gentry back to Forest Street. We can always claim she was nervous and upset and didn't want to go there on her own."

"I get it." Smythe rose to his feet. "That way, we can 'ave Wiggins and Hatchet at the ready if the inspector is delayed."

"Correct. If I'm right, Phillip Eddington is a killer. I don't want Miss Gentry at that house alone with him next door. This way, we'll have a good excuse for them being there with her when the inspector arrives."

Wiggins and Hatchet got up and the three of them turned to go. "Take Fred with you," Mrs. Jeffries insisted. "For what I've got in mind, he'll come in handy."

Fred, who'd been curled up in disgrace under Wiggins's chair, came wiggling out as he heard his name. His tail thumped against the kitchen floor.

"Come on, boy." Wiggins called the dog.

"And be sure and have Miss Gentry bring Miranda as well. If her nose is as good as I think it is, she's going to catch our killer for us." If Mrs. Jeffries was wrong, they might all end up disgraced. But that was a risk she was willing to take to stop a murderer from leaving the country.

"Anything else?" Smythe asked.

Mrs. Jeffries thought for a moment. She wanted to make sure she hadn't forgotten anything important. "Yes, when Miss Gentry gets to Forest Street, have her and the dog go directly to the garden. That's very important. Miranda and Fred both need to be out there when the inspector arrives. That may be the only way this situation is going to work."

"What about Eddington?" Smythe asked. "Should we keep an eye on him?" He didn't see how they could, but if it was necessary, he'd think of something.

"No, don't worry. Even if he leaves the premises when he sees the inspector, he won't get far. Not once the police have the evidence I pray is there."

"Uh, Mrs. Jeffries, what's Miss Gentry to say when the inspector asks why it was so urgent she meet him?" Wiggins asked.

Mrs. Jeffries smiled. "She's to tell him she's fairly sure she knows why someone was trying to kill her."

"And why's that?" Hatchet prompted. Like the rest of them, he was curious.

"Because someone didn't want Miranda in the communal garden. That's where the bodies are buried, you see. Miranda is actually quite good at digging up corpses. She's got the best nose in London."

"Miss Gentry's not home," Martha explained. "She's taken Miranda out for a walk."

"Cor blimey," Wiggins muttered. "That's all we need. Our plan'll be ruined."

"What's this about, then?" Martha asked suspiciously. "Why do you need Miss Gentry? You're not goin' to arrest her, are you?"

"We're not the police, Martha," Smythe retorted. "We're tryin' to 'elp 'er. Besides, why would the police be wantin' to arrest 'er anyway?"

"Don't pay me any mind, I'm acting like a goose. I expect I'm rattled over what happened." Martha made a disgusted face. "Them two sisters of hers was by early this morning. They was saying all sorts of nasty things. They said Miss Gentry's goin' to get in trouble for making false claims to the police about someone wanting to kill her. They caused quite a ruckus, they did. They was shouting and carrying on so loudly that Miranda started barking. Mind you, I think the dog knew them hags was tormenting

292

Miss Gentry and that was her way of gettin' shut of them. Mind you, I —"

"Do you know when Miss Gentry is due back?" Hatchet interrupted. Annabeth Gentry's domestic troubles were not of paramount importance at this moment. Finding her was.

Martha scowled. She didn't like being interrupted. "She didn't say when she'd be back," she snapped.

"Do you know where she went, then?" Smythe pressed. "It's urgent that we find her. We think we've found out who's been trying to kill her."

Martha gaped at him. "Why didn't you say that in the first place? I don't know exactly where she's gone, but I do know her usual walking spots. She's either gone to the footpath this side of the scrubs —"

"Why would she go there? Isn't that where Miranda found Porter's corpse?" Wiggins asked incredulously. "Seems to me if someone is tryin' to kill you, you don't go walking all on your own in lonely places."

"I said she *might* have gone there," Martha replied tartly. "But she's probably over at the commons." She waved her hand in the general direction of Shepherd's Bush Green. "If she's not there, try the footpath. If she's not at either of them places, then I don't know where she is."

"Thanks, Martha," Smythe said. "If she comes home, tell her to stay right here. It's urgent we find her."

They dashed back to the carriage. "What'll we do if we can't find her?" Wiggins asked.

"We'll find her," Smythe promised. "Mark my words, we'll find her."

"I hope she's all right," Hatchet said. He looked a bit worried. "You don't think she could have possibly come to some harm, do you?" He didn't need to remind the others that their involvement in this case had started because someone was trying to kill Miss Gentry.

"Of course not," Smythe said, but the thought had crossed his mind.

But their fears turned out to be for naught, as they found her less than five minutes later walking up the Uxbridge Road toward home.

Within twenty minutes, they'd explained what had to be done, and Smythe, after dropping them off, was on his way to find the inspector.

"I say, Smythe," Witherspoon began as he and Barnes climbed out of the carriage,

"Miss Gentry didn't happen to explain why it was so urgent I meet her here, did she?"

Smythe shook his head. "No sir, she only said it were right important. Said it were a matter of life and death and that you'd know what she meant."

As instructed, he'd brought the inspector and Barnes to Miss Gentry's house on Forest Street. He only hoped the housekeeper was right about everything and they wouldn't end up looking incredibly foolish.

"Well, I can't say that I do," Witherspoon murmured. "But as I was coming over here anyway, it doesn't matter."

"You were comin' 'ere, sir?" Smythe deliberately kept the question casual. "That's a bit of a coincidence, isn't it?"

"Not really. You see we found out this morning that Mr. Eddington was one of the names Stan McIntosh gave as a reference to get his job at the school. I'm a bit curious as to why Mr. Eddington never mentioned that to us and as to why he lied."

"We don't know that he did lie, sir," Barnes pointed out. "Maybe McIntosh was the one lying about the school being sold. Take a look at that, sir." He pointed toward the front garden of number one, Eddington's house.

"Gracious, it's a 'For Sale' sign. Mr. Eddington never mentioned he was selling his house." Witherspoon didn't like this. He didn't like it one bit. First the lie and now this. He was beginning to think that perhaps Mr. Eddington wasn't what he appeared to be. "I do believe we ought to have a word with him right now." He started toward the walkway to number one.

"But, sir," Smythe yelled, "don't you think we ought to see if Miss Gentry's all right first? She was in a bit of state when she came to the 'ouse, sir. That's why Mrs. Jeffries insisted that Wiggins and Hatchet come back here with 'er. They didn't think she ought to be alone."

Witherspoon hesitated. "Yes, yes, of course you're right. We must see to the lady." He started toward the open front door of number two.

"It was right convenient that Wiggins and Mr. Hatchet were there when Miss Gentry showed up, wasn't it?" Barnes said as they fell in step behind the inspector.

Smythe swallowed. The constable was no fool. "Luty and Hatchet had dropped by to 'ave tea," he said. "They come to visit quite often."

"So I've noticed," Barnes replied. They walked up the steps and into the foyer. The place was obviously still being redone. Paint buckets and ladders cluttered the long hallway leading to the back of the house. Drop cloths were scattered about the floors and the scent of fire hung heavily in the air. "They always seem to be around when the inspector's about to solve a case."

They crossed the huge, empty kitchen and reached the back door. "Uh, yeah," Smythe said. He didn't know what to say next. "It's right fortunate, innit?"

Barnes laughed softly. "Don't look so worried, man. I think the inspector's a very lucky man to have such a devoted staff."

Smythe breathed a sigh of relief as they came out into the garden. There was a small, paved terrace outside the kitchen that ran for ten feet on either side of the door. Beyond that was the garden proper. Annabeth Gentry, Hatchet, and Wiggins were standing in the middle of the grass.

Miranda, nose to the ground, was following some sort of trail. Fred was sniffing the ground behind her.

"Hello, Inspector," Annabeth called, waving to him. "Thank you so much for coming."

From the corner of his eye, Smythe saw Miranda circling a patch of dirt at the far edge of the grass. The spot was just under a tree, near the back wall.

He glanced at Miss Gentry and the others. If they'd done as they were instructed, they'd probably arrived here only a few minutes ahead of them. He'd dropped them off at Orley Road and told them to wait an hour before going into the garden. He'd needed the time to find the inspector and get him over here.

"Good day, Miss Gentry, I understand you wanted to see me," Witherspoon said. "The constable and I came as soon as we got your message." For the life of him, he couldn't see anything that looked the least dangerous.

"Thank you, Inspector." Annabeth's smile faltered a bit. She looked at Wiggins. "It was good of you to come so quickly. I'm very grateful."

It was at that moment that Miranda started to dig.

Chapter 11

The inspector waited politely for Miss Gentry to continue speaking. She merely smiled at him.

"Hello, sir," Wiggins called.

"Inspector." Hatchet smiled and nodded. "Nice to see you, sir."

Bewildered, Witherspoon glanced around the garden. What on earth was this about? There certainly didn't seem to be anything going on here that could be construed as a matter of life and death. Except for the fact that Miranda appeared to be digging quite a large hole, the day was extraordinarily quiet. "Uh, Miss Gentry, from what I understand, you seemed to feel something was very much amiss this morning."

"That's quite right, Inspector, I did." She smiled and glanced toward the two dogs. Her snout deep in the hole, Miranda was digging furiously. Fred, his nose less than an inch from the ground, was circling the area in a rapid figure-eight sort of motion. "You see, I suddenly had an idea."

"An idea," the inspector prompted. "What kind of idea?"

Barnes was now watching the dogs.

"Well, uh, about why someone might be trying to kill me. You see, it all started with me finding that fellow's body."

The dirt stopped flying out of the hole and Miranda buried her snout in the ground. She grabbed something between her teeth.

Fred began circling and crept up close to the other dog. His whole body went rigid.

Witherspoon, not noticing the dogs, kept his attention on Miss Gentry. "Yes, I know that. We're quite certain the threats on your life are connected to Tim Porter."

"But that's just it, sir," she began slowly. She was trying to say it just right. Mrs. Jeffries's instructions had been very explicit. "I don't think they're connected to this Porter business at all." She broke off and pointed behind the inspector. "Look, there's my neighbor Mr. Eddington."

Eddington had stepped out onto his terrace. His gaze raked the garden, taking in the two policemen, Miss Gentry, and the others, and then he spotted the dogs. A look of horror spread across his face.

"I say, Mr. Eddington," Witherspoon called to him. "I'd like a word with you, sir.

I'll pop over in a few minutes, if that's all right."

But Eddington didn't answer. He turned on his heel and bolted back to the house. Smythe started as though he meant to go after him, but Barnes held up his hand and whispered, "Wait. Do nothing yet."

"How rude," Witherspoon muttered, and turned his attention back to Miss Gentry. "I'm sorry. Uh, what were you saying? Something about digging up Porter's body . . ."

But Annabeth Gentry wasn't paying any attention to the inspector. She was gaping at Miranda. The dog had wrestled something out of the ground and was gripping it between her teeth. But the object was buried deep, and despite the dog's efforts, it wouldn't come all the way out.

Fred, seeing the brown, dirt-covered thing in Miranda's mouth, barked jealously and charged the bloodhound in an effort to get her to share. Miranda dropped it and growled at Fred.

"Oh dear," Witherspoon exclaimed. "We can't have this. Whatever's the matter? What's wrong with those two? It's not like Fred to be so aggressive." Afraid that his beloved dog would get bitten, the inspector charged across the grass. "Come on now,

Fred, back off. Whatever it is Miranda's found, it's hers." He got close to the animals and stopped dead. "Oh, my good gracious!" he cried. "Constable, you'd best come help. Wiggins, call Fred back. Miss Gentry, call Miranda. Get them away from that thing immediately!"

"What is it, sir?" Barnes had already started across the scruffy grass.

"It's a human arm, Constable, and from what I can see here, it appears to be attached to a body."

It was well past dinnertime by the time Smythe, Wiggins, and Hatchet returned to Upper Edmonton Gardens. They told the women what had happened.

"It were ever so exciting," Wiggins said. "By the time they finished this evening, that dog 'ad found three bodies. Fred 'elped, a bit. Well, 'e tried to. But the inspector kept 'olding him back."

"Only three?" Mrs. Jeffries asked. "Thank goodness. I was afraid there would be far more."

Smythe looked at the women suspiciously. "You're all mighty calm about this. What's goin' on? 'Ave you been up to somethin'?"

"We didn't sit here twiddlin' our thumbs

while you all was gone, that's for sure," Luty said. "After Hepzibah told us who she thought the killer was, we finished puttin' the rest of the puzzle together. Betsy and I went over to Hampton House, to see my friend Skidmore —"

"You mean Lord Skidmore," Hatchet interrupted. He looked at the men. "He owns majority shares in a number of steamship lines. For some odd reason, he finds Madam quite amusing."

"He likes me." Luty grinned. "What's more, he's fast, discreet, and he knows how to do a body a favor."

Betsy giggled. "He got us the information we needed right away and he gave us tea."

Smythe's eyes narrowed. "What kind of information could 'e give ya? Oh, I git it, did 'e know anything about that ticket we found in Deborah Baker's things?"

"That and more," Luty replied. "It's amazin' what you can learn by lookin' at a manifest. There's no record of a Deborah Baker on that voyage of the *Laura Gibbens* last year."

"Does that mean she wasn't on the ship?"

"We think she traveled under another name," Mrs. Jeffries said. "A married name. You see, there wasn't a Deborah Baker on that vessel, but there was a Mr. and Mrs. Phillip Essex on board. I'm willing to bet Phillip Essex is really Phillip Eddington."

"Cor blimey," Wiggins muttered. "I'll bet she's one of them women buried in his back garden."

"Probably," Luty said. "But that ain't all we learned. We also found out that Eddington and McIntosh go way back. They'd known each other since McIntosh was a steward. Eddington was a passenger on at least three of McIntosh's voyages. Now you fellas finish your story. We're not tryin' to steal your thunder."

"Hmm, madam, I suspect that's precisely what you're trying to do," Hatchet replied. He looked at Mrs. Jeffries. "Perhaps you'd be so kind as to tell us how you figured it out. I'm afraid that even with the discovery of the bodies, I still don't see how it's all connected."

"Neither did I until Fred dug up Mrs. Goodge's daffodil bulbs," Mrs. Jeffries replied. "That's when it all fell into place."

"What's them bulbs got to do with it?" Wiggins asked.

Mrs. Jeffries laughed and poured herself another cup of tea. "It wasn't the bulbs that were important, it was the digging. That's what I finally realized this morning. You see, it wasn't Porter's murder that precipitated the attempts on Miss Gentry's life, it was her dog digging up his body. Once I started from that point, from the fact that it was the dog that was a threat to someone, and not Miss Gentry, then it all made sense."

"Tell them how you figured out it was Eddington," Mrs. Goodge prompted.

"He was the only person it could be," Mrs. Jeffries said. "If he'd just been content with trying to kill Miss Gentry, we'd never have figured it out. But it was the sabotage to her new home that pointed the finger directly at him."

"I don't understand," Smythe said.

"I asked myself why would anyone sabotage a house, and there was only one reason. To keep someone from moving into it? But someone already lived on Forest Street and nothing was happening to him —"

"I get it," Wiggins interrupted. "That means he must be the one doin' the sabotagin'."

"Right. He is the only person who lives on Forest Street and he wants to keep it that way. Once Porter's body was found,

Eddington realized that he was in grave danger if Miss Gentry and her bloodhound moved into their new home. He did everything in his power to keep Miranda out of that garden. He even had a confrontation with Miss Gentry to try and get her to agree to keep the dog on a lead."

"Now we know why," Betsy said. "He didn't want her digging up what he'd buried there."

Mrs. Jeffries took a quick sip of tea. "I was sure that Eddington was the killer, but I didn't know why until today. After Luty and Betsy told me about seeing that name on the manifest, I had an idea it must have something to do with killing for profit. But I'm still not sure how he managed it."

"Well, he killed at least three women," Hatchet said slowly. "At least that was the body count before we left this afternoon."

"Where was Eddington?" Mrs. Jeffries asked.

"He scarpered," Smythe answered. "Good thing 'e did, too. It were 'im takin' off like that that convinced the inspector 'e's the killer."

"That and the fact that Miss Gentry insisted he's the one that's been trying to keep her out of the house on Forest Street," Hatchet added.

306

"Do they have any idea where he's gone?"

"Probably to the train station," Smythe said. "I managed to whisper to Miss Gentry to tell the inspector she'd gotten suspicious of Eddington and followed him to Cook's. She told the inspector she'd watched him buy that steamship ticket." He didn't add that he was sure Constable Barnes had overheard him. He'd share that little nugget with the others later.

"I only hope the inspector manages to catch the fellow before he gets out of the country," Mrs. Jeffries said. "We can't let him get away. He's evil. Absolutely evil."

"The inspector will get 'im, Mrs. Jeffries," Smythe assured her. "Now, you still 'aven't told us everything. 'Ow you knew it were him behind everything. Did 'e kill Porter and McIntosh?"

"He probably killed McIntosh," she said. "But I'm fairly certain McIntosh killed Porter. Your source was right, Smythe, Porter probably was blackmailing McIntosh. Do you recall Father Jerridan telling Hatchet about tramps sleeping in the entryway of St. Matthew's Church? We think it must have been Porter and that he witnessed McIntosh and Eddington burying one of the bodies in the garden. We'll never know for certain, of course, but it does make sense. It would explain Porter's bragging that there was more money coming his way."

"Especially if McIntosh paid him off a time or two so he'd let his guard down," Betsy put in. "It'd be easier to lure him up that footpath if he wasn't suspicious of you."

"Why did he have that purse on him?" Smythe wondered.

"We think he must've slipped into the garden after they'd buried the body and dug it up," Mrs. Goodge said. She didn't want to be left out just because she'd not gone with Luty and Betsy. "You know, so he'd have something real to wave under McIntosh's nose."

"Why do you think he approached McIntosh?" Hatchet asked. "Why not Eddington?" He still wasn't clear on a number of things, but he was patient.

"He probably thought McIntosh would be easier. He probably didn't have the nerve to go knocking on Eddington's front door. He'd be much more comfortable going after someone of his own class. Besides, remember what happened to Smythe at the White Hare pub," Betsy explained. "Porter went there asking questions about

McIntosh. Maybe we'll never know for sure, but he went to McIntosh instead of Eddington."

Smythe smiled at Betsy and then turned to Mrs. Jeffries. "All right, if McIntosh killed Porter to keep his mouth shut, why would Eddington kill McIntosh? If your theory is right and they'd known each other for years, why would Eddington want to kill 'im now?"

"We're not certain," Mrs. Jeffries replied. "But I suspect it's because Eddington decided to move on."

"He didn't just put his house on the market today," Mrs. Goodge interjected. "One of my sources told me he'd been to see the estate agent toward the middle of August, just a few days after Porter's body was found."

"So he killed McIntosh so there wouldn't be any loose ends about?" Wiggins frowned in confusion. "But why was Eddington killing women in the first place? That's what I want to know."

"I have an idea," Mrs. Jeffries said, "but we won't know for sure about his motives until we hear what the inspector has to say." She glanced anxiously at the clock. "I do hope that Eddington didn't catch a train to the coast. They'll have a devil of a time catching the fellow if he gets out of the country."

They caught Eddington as he tried to board a train for Southampton. He saw them coming, and for a moment Witherspoon thought he might make a run for it.

But he didn't. Perhaps it was the dozen men converging on the platform that convinced him he hadn't a hope of escape.

Eddington smiled slightly but said nothing as Witherspoon and Barnes approached. A porter, halfway down the train steps to the platform, saw the police and quickly disappeared inside. Gentlemen in top hats grabbed their ladies and stepped out of the way as the police constables made a wide circle around their quarry.

The train whistle shrilled just as they reached him. The inspector waited for quiet. "Phillip Eddington, you're under arrest for murder," Witherspoon said somberly. "Constable, take him into custody."

Barnes pulled out his handcuffs. Eddington sighed, dropped his bag, and held out his wrists. "I'm surprised you caught me," he said conversationally, still smiling at Witherspoon. "You struck me as being a bit dim."

"You were wrong," Barnes said. He finished cuffing Eddington and then knelt down next to the bag the criminal had been carrying. It was a large black leather traveling case with a wide silver clasp. "What's this, then? Shall I open it, Inspector?"

"Yes," Witherspoon replied. He wondered why people always underestimated him. But then again, perhaps it wasn't a bad thing. After all, Eddington had been caught. But being thought a dim sort of fellow wasn't very pleasant. The inspector pushed that silly notion out of his mind. He'd concentrate on the task at hand.

Barnes pushed the clasp. "It's locked." Eddington still continued to smile. The constable reached up and stuck his hand into the man's coat pocket. He pulled out a handful of bills, some coins, and a small silver key. He handed the bills and coins to another police constable. "Make sure this is logged in properly." Then he knelt down, unlocked the case, and gave a long, low whistle. "It looks like Mr. Eddington was preparing for a long trip. The case is full of money, sir. Five- and ten-pound notes."

"Let's get him down to the station," Witherspoon said, "and see what he has to say for himself."

"I've nothing to say, Inspector," Eddington told him calmly. "Absolutely nothing."

It was well past eleven that night before the inspector arrived home. As he'd seen the kitchen lamps from the street, he went to that room first. "Gracious" — he stopped just inside the door and stared at the crowd around his table — "you're all here."

" 'Course we are," Luty said firmly. "We want to know what happened. You can't have something exciting like diggin' up bodies happen and then expect us to go home without findin' out if you caught that Eddington feller."

They all watched him carefully. He looked dreadfully tired, but he didn't appear to be annoyed. As a matter of fact, he looked almost pleased. "That sounds reasonable. I expect I'd be dying of curiosity myself. I say, is there anything to eat? I'm famished."

Mrs. Goodge, who'd been almost asleep before the inspector arrived, got to her feet. "I've got some nice buns right here, sir." She pulled a covered plate off the counter and slid it onto the table. Mrs. Jeffries, who'd slipped out of her chair when she heard him coming, said, "Do sit down and have some tea, sir. Let me pour you a cup."

"That would be lovely." He sat down and waited for them to finish preparing his snack. He picked up a bun and took a huge bite. "That's wonderful," he said as soon as he'd swallowed. "I expect you're wondering what happened."

"That's why we waited here half the night," Luty replied. She didn't want to rush him, but she did wish he'd get on with it.

"We arrested Phillip Eddington at the train station," Witherspoon said. "At first he refused to tell us anything at all. But when we confronted him with all the evidence we had against him, he confessed."

"Three bodies is a lot of evidence," Hatchet said grimly. He closed his eyes and shuddered. Watching them being dug out of the ground this afternoon had been quite gruesome.

"Oh, it wasn't the bodies," Witherspoon said. "It was the marriage licenses. The fellow had quite a collection of them at the bottom of his bag. In the past fifteen years, he's married and murdered seven different women." He shook his head in disbelief.

"Good gracious, sir. I thought there was

only three bodies," Mrs. Goodge ex-claimed.

"Three bodies at the house in Forest Street," the inspector replied. "But there's four more buried at his home in Halifax. We've wired the Canadian authorities. We're waiting to hear back from them about what they find."

"Cor blimey, 'ow'd 'e get away with that?"

"To hear him tell it" — Witherspoon sighed — "it was very easy. Eddington was careful when he picked his victims. He'd find a woman who had money and no rela-tives. After a short courtship, he'd propose marriage and the lady would agree. But as part of his proposal, he'd tell his victim that he had to go back to England to manage his estate, or, if the victim was English, that he had to return to Canada to manage the family business. The unlucky woman would generally give him her money to take to his bankers because, after all, she wasn't going to be coming back. Once he had their cash, they'd sail off for either England or Canada. He always made sure he arrived in London in the dead of night. He wanted to be certain no one saw him. Before the poor woman re-alized what was happening, he'd cosh her over the head and then strangle her to finish the job." He broke off and shook his head sadly. "Poor ladies. They never stood a chance. Then, with the help of Stan McIntosh, he'd bury them in the garden. His plan worked perfectly."

"But that's monstrous!" Hatchet cried. "Surely someone must have suspected he was up to something?"

"Who was there to suspect?" the inspector asked. "He made sure his victims were somewhat alone in the world and he always made sure he arrived in either Halifax or London late at night so that no one ever spotted him with his wife."

"But what about the ship? Surely people on the ship noticed him and his wife."

"He used an assumed name. But that wasn't quite as foolproof as he hoped. He admitted that's how he and McIntosh started working together. Eddington always traveled on different steamship lines, but he didn't realize that the staff frequently moved from one line to another. He had to cut McIntosh in on the scheme when McIntosh recognized him from an earlier trip on another vessel."

"I'm amazed he's gotten away with it for so long." Mrs. Goodge clucked her tongue. "Fifteen years. Seven women. That's awful.

Didn't any of them have friends or relatives that inquired about them?"

"He took care of that," Witherspoon said. "As I said, Stan McIntosh was his accomplice. We found a box of postcards under McIntosh's bed. We're fairly certain that McIntosh used those cards to send off to the victims' friends. Pretending to be the victim, he'd write those cards and send them off. Her friends would receive cards saying married life was wonderful and she couldn't be happier."

"But how could McIntosh do that? People know each other's handwriting," Betsy said.

Witherspoon smiled sadly. "We've done some checking. McIntosh served three years in jail in New York for forgery."

"But didn't these people ever write back?"

"Of course. Eddington gave the women he duped the wrong address. He used the Helmsley Grammar School address as his own. They, in turn, gave that address to their friends before they left. McIntosh intercepted the letters."

Mrs. Jeffries nodded. That explained why McIntosh wouldn't let anyone else get the mail. "Didn't people get suspicious when the cards stopped coming?"

"Possibly. But not enough to do anything

about it. He was counting on the fact that we live in a busy, impersonal world. People come and go so much more than they used to. They drift apart. Remember, he picked women who hadn't any close relatives. He was bragging about that, about how clever he was to pick people that no one really cared about." Witherspoon closed his eyes briefly. "He used the newspapers to refine his search. He'd read the obituaries and probate news to see who'd died and left an estate. He hunted his victims on both sides of the Atlantic with the cunning and malice of the devil himself. He took ruthless advantage of women who were alone in the world and without anyone to see to their safety. But he wasn't quite as clever as he thought; several people had started making inquiries."

"Poor Miss Gentry. Lucky she didn't become one of his victims," Mrs. Goodge said.

"She was lucky, indeed," Witherspoon agreed. "He admitted trying to kill her. He stole a coach and tried to run her down. When that didn't work, he had McIntosh chuck those bricks off the wall at her head. He couldn't afford for Miranda to start nosing around in his garden. Not with all those bodies."

"Why not just kill the dog?" Hatchet asked.

"Constable Barnes asked him that," the inspector replied. "He said he'd tried. But that he couldn't get close enough to the animal to do it any harm."

"Why didn't he move the bodies?" Luty asked.

"He couldn't. Not with the workmen coming and going at Miss Gentry's place. Especially after the vandalism. The builder had someone staying there some nights. Eddington couldn't be sure he wouldn't be seen." He sighed deeply. "The man is a monster, and God forgive me for saying it, but I'm glad he's going to hang. I thank the Lord we caught him before he could hurt anyone else."

"*You* caught him, sir," Mrs. Jeffries said gently. She could see he was very affected by the horror of this case. For that matter, now that they'd heard the gruesome details, they were all horrified as well. "Why don't you go up to bed, sir. You look exhausted."

"I *am* tired." He got up and gave them a tired smile. "I want to thank all of you for your help. You did right in taking care of Miss Gentry today. I shudder to think what would have happened if she'd gone to that garden alone."

A bit guilty, they all glanced at one another, but the inspector didn't appear to notice. "I believe we should all have a bit of a holiday when this is over," he continued. "Perhaps we'll go to the country."

"That would be lovely, sir," Mrs. Jeffries replied.

He started for the back stairs. Fred left Wiggins and trotted after the inspector. Perhaps he sensed the man needed a bit of comfort.

"Excuse me, sir," Mrs. Jeffries said. "Was Eddington responsible for the poisoned cream that Miranda ate?"

"He says he wasn't and he's no reason to lie. He's going to hang anyway. Admitting one more attempt on Miss Gentry's life won't make any difference in his sentence." He smiled sadly and continued toward the stairs.

"Thank you, sir. Good night." Mrs. Jeffries turned to the others. "Well, what a horrifying story this has turned out to be."

"No, it woulda only been really awful if that varmint had got away with it and went on to kill a bunch more women." Luty got up. "Let's get goin', Hatchet. You're fallin' asleep in your chair."

"I most certainly am not." He tossed

Luty a quick frown and then looked at Mrs. Jeffries. "What about that poisoned cream? If Eddington didn't do it, who did?"

"One of her relatives, I expect," Mrs. Jeffries mused.

"What are we going to do, then?" Betsy asked. "They might try again."

"Not if we tell her," the housekeeper replied. "She can make it very clear to her family that in the event of her death, there's to be a full police investigation. I don't think they'll have another go at her. Not now. They've had the police around once. They'll probably be too frightened to try it again. But just to be on the safe side, I believe we'll have her mention that she's a number of friends who will raise quite a fuss if she disappears or comes to harm."

"Good," Mrs. Goodge said stoutly. "That's what we've all got to do. Especially us women who are alone in the world. We've got to keep an eye out for one another. That's the only way any of us will be safe."

"Amen to that, Mrs. Goodge," Mrs. Jeffries agreed. "Amen to that."